The Enlightened Barista

By Frank Elaridi

NICOIA -

thANK you FOR AllowiNg me to co-cReAte w/ you! you ARe tRuly aN ANgel, build & they will come ☺ I'M glAd I followed your soul iNto this lifetime.   — FRANKiP (2016)

Testimonials for
The Enlightened Barista

"As Frank takes us on a pilgrimage from the mountains of Lebanon to spiritual India, following the journey of a barista in search of truth, we remember an ancient memory hidden within our hearts. By the end, you may find yourself accidentally enlightened."
-Sonia Choquette, New York Times best-selling author of "Walking Home: A pilgrimage from humbled to healed"

"Frank Elaridi is a brilliant and entertaining story teller. *The Enlightened Barista* divinely guides us on a journey of healing and awakening; and in the process we discover our Soul."
-Davidji, Former Dean of the Chopra Center and author of "Secrets of Meditation"

He who uses force forfeits his own power.

Only fear that which can hurt you.
And nothing can hurt you.

A Nightingale and a Boy

A beardless boy sat on a stump, looking back at his life with piercing regret. With a prayer of desperation on his lips, he cried:

"Oh Lord, full of love and mercy, I was born a human boy, with a tendency to surrender to slumber. But had I been born a nightingale, I would rise as the moon throws his glow upon the field and perch myself on the highest tree below the stars: patches of light sewn into a dark carpet. And there I would sit in perfect meditation.

"I would fly effortlessly among the houses and sing the song of God with a heavenly chirp.

"This feeble body is useless for worship, but had I only been born a nightingale, I could live off a simple diet of worm and seeds and be truly auspicious."

As he was having this thought, A Nightingale sat on a branch above him and declared:

"Many times my soul has warned of doubt in my heart! I am but a stupid Nightingale, but had I been born a human boy I would rise every morning as the sun spills his rays and I would meditate in stillness.

"I would use my arms and legs to climb the highest mountain top and sit in perfect Lotus posture, which my wings and fickle legs do not allow me to do now.

"I am only a simple bird and this modest nest is my only possession, but had I only been born a human boy, then I could live on a steady diet of fruits and vegetables, and I would not eat worms, for it pains my soul to harm them.

"If I were only a human boy, I would truly be able to worship."

And so the nightingale and the boy went on with their lives, both wishing to be the other while postponing their inevitable walk along the path to enlightenment.

Foreword

A Course in Miracles begins with a simple declaration, that it is a required course, and the only voluntary part is the time you choose to take it. There are many factors that contribute to delaying the work, but for most it's just that: it takes work. Aside from the 365 lessons, one for each day of the year, there is also a rather lengthy supplementary reading and teacher's manual to go along with it. For many, that can be an intimidating endeavor. The Enlightened Barista is a fictional approach to A Course in Miracles, and as we see Matias awaken, we learn what waking means.

The Enlightened Barista is not meant to replace A Course in Miracles, for what it is cannot be replaced. Rather, it is intended to gently introduce you to some of the lessons I have found to be useful for me, in the form of an entertaining story.

The curriculum in A Course in Miracles emphasizes application of the lessons rather than theory, and so I wanted The Enlightened Barista to be a story that shows you how you can apply these lessons in everyday life situations.

The ego has no desire other than to fulfill itself. You can float aimlessly like a fallen feather to appease it, or soar like the nightingale to appease yourself. As you embark on this adventure, you will hear occasional mention of silencing the ego, a that triumph Matias, like the rest of us, must make. The Course offers a simple tool to help us silence the ego when it speaks. It says, "Whenever you question your value, say 'God Himself is incomplete without me.' Remember this when the ego speaks and you will not hear it." I practice this on a regular basis, reminding myself that the ego voice is not mine- I am the observer. The ego, in its madness, does not even realize that it is insane. When it speaks, we believe it, even though its voice attempts to shatter the kingdom of Heaven within us, just as a strong tide lays waste to a sand castle on the shore.

Truth is the theme of the story, but forgiveness is the key. One of my favorite lessons in A Course in Miracles is "God does not forgive, because He has never condemned." Matias is robbed and abandoned in one instant and watches his life plan fall apart in another, but he must learn to forgive if he wants to see the world as it really is.

The reason Matias is able to attain enlightenment at all, is because he approaches the Great Guru with the confession that he doesn't know anything. When we think we know, we cannot learn, because we shut truth out. When we recognize that we do not know what anything is for, we leave an open window for truth to enter and teach us what it would have us learn. That is why I think it is so important that the first few lessons in the Course are centered around the recognition that we do not know what anything is for nor what anything really means. Only then can we open ourselves up to receive.

In Raphael, the nomad who first tells Matias about the Great Guru in India, we see a reflection of the ego. Like Raphael, the ego searches for truth and love endlessly, under one condition: don't ever find it. Because if you knew unconditional love, you would realize that you have no need for the ego, for it has misguided you all along.

With inspiration from the Tao and yogic teachings from the Kundalini tradition woven into the text, The Enlightened Barista reminds us of our truth and calls out our ancient memory from its hiding place within our hearts.

This book teaches us to be soft, while the world constantly tempts us to be hard. We are all perfect, loving beings. If you are not that way now, then at some point in your life, someone taught you otherwise. The whole point of spirituality is to unlearn what you have been taught by parents and other authority figures who were only doing the best they could with what they knew.

Some people tell me they think it is arrogant to believe they are perfect and holy. I think it's arrogant to think you are not. You see, God has already declared you are perfect like Him, and every day the universe obeys your thoughts and manifests them for you. So to think you are not a perfect and holy creator, is saying that you know better than God and the universe what you really are- and that is arrogance.

The course teaches that the ego is confused about the meaning of giving and receiving. It thinks that only by hoarding its possessions does it attain wealth, but the spirit understands that only by giving do we truly receive. So with peace and joy, this story is the gift that I would lay upon the lap of humanity, that I may have God's peace and joy as my own.

There are enough lessons in A Course in Miracles to line the entire way to Heaven. Although this book only emphasizes a selection of them, understanding even one lesson fully, has the power to awaken you to the truth of what you really are.

As you follow Matias on his journey from a lost youth to a teacher of truth, let stillness fall upon you. Remember that the past is a dream, and the future imagined; for what it's worth, this is the story of The Enlightened Barista.

Chapter 1

The barista drew an imprint of a rose in the foam in the cup of expresso, but no one would notice it. The customer would drink it without ever taking a moment to admire his masterpiece.

A mascot for his country, his hair was as dark as the rocks surrounding the Mediterranean coastline and his eyes shaded evergreen like the Biblical cedars in the ancient mountains, so full of magic and dignity.

He hoped that maybe just this once someone would order something other than expresso or mate, the drink every native of the Lebanese mountains will claim as their national drink although it came from the Argentineans long ago. Just as he was having this thought, two more orders came in: one for expresso and another for mate.

Nothing ever changed. Each cup he brewed wounded his spirit.

He wondered if perhaps he should have gone to school like his father insisted. Matias did rather enjoy grade school while he was there. Not so much the education itself, but the communion of friends, a gathering of people in a single place five days a week—there was a sense of security in that. Perhaps it mirrored his inner longing for stability in life. That was something he inherited from his mother, as well as her tall, thin frame. He particularly missed the lectures about religion which were held in the school cathedral, because he felt as though he were learning something secretive and sacred. The cold, dark cathedral added to the mystery and made him feel as though he was a member of some selective society, involved in some secret ritual.

But college meant math and the only thing Matias was interested in counting was his money. Four years he had been working at the coffee shop, saving every lira he earned. Four is such a small number. It's the average amount of years a person spends in college. It's the number of petals on a four-leaf clover. Even babies count to four: One, two, three, four. Four years is such a short time. It's an eternity.

But every year was worth it, because one day he would have enough money to purchase a villa in the nice part of the village next to Monsieur Jumblatt's extravagant home and all the sheiks would take refuge in his garden. Jumblatt came into the coffee shop every morning wearing an Italian suit with an assistant by his side. He always ordered the same thing. Cappuccino. Extra foam.

Jumblatt, who came from a wealthy family and was always happy to recite events that dealt with his forefathers, had studied in France and built a real estate empire. God was fair to the Jumblatt family. He gave them very little in the intellect department, and not one of them had enough humility to fill an ounce of a cup, but He gave them style. And style, Matias thought, was everything. It moves a person, helps them cross the street, wakes them up in the morning. Monsieur Jumblatt was a man of taste and sophistication, and Matias was determined to be like him.

Matias himself had good taste, and he often got complimented for the way his shirts matched his pants perfectly. But he longed for an Italian suit like Monsieur Jumblatt's. Longing has delicate, warm hands, but a tight grip that grasps the heart and makes it throb with anguish.

It was the very same summer when Matias was hired to work in the coffee shop that he first realized he wanted a villa like Jumblatt's. He was sent to the marvelous place to deliver crates filled with the finest Italian roasted coffee beans for Jumblatt to serve to his houseguests. A tall brick fence and a wall of giant trees surrounded every corner of the villa, hiding it away like a prince in his palace. The wait staff asked Matias to wait on a sofa in the main living room of the first floor while the kitchen staff unloaded the coffee beans from his car and the head butler brought him money for the supply. As he waited, Matias peeked around a few of the rooms and wound up in the lobby, but saw quickly how easy it would be to get lost. Matias felt like Theseus navigating through the Minotaur's Labyrinth. He didn't want to get fired from his new job so soon after he started, and went back to the living room to sit on the sofa in the same exact spot he was earlier, as though someone would realize that he had moved even an inch. One of the living room walls suddenly shifted and two servants came out of their hidden quarters. They set plates of pistachios and fruits on the table beside Matias, and asked him what he wanted to drink. Matias was fascinated by the whole thing. He had a few well-to-do relatives, but nothing like that, with servants literally coming out of the walls. He decided that day that the rest of his working years would be dedicated to saving up for a villa of his own, right next door, where *his* servants would serve Jumblatt pistachios and fruit and offer *him* a drink.

In the meantime, he was a frustrated prisoner with the notion of being trapped in one body, at one point in time, when there were so many other bodies he would never get to be. He looked at all the customers in the shop that day and was bitter at the thought that each one of them had seen a painting he would never see or heard a song that he would never hear and that feeling of not being able to be everywhere at once was a tiny little knife hidden in the wires of his heart. Even Madame Salman, in all her fatness, had a gross obesity that he would never get to know, representing yet another thing he wouldn't get to experience before he died.

Truth be told, it was not the most exciting thing in the world to be a barista. There were a dozen other jobs Matias could do, being witty and young and so full of ambition. But none of those other things would introduce him to so many interesting people with interesting stories. Each face was a book, with a beginning, middle and an end. He met a ballerina from France who told him about the glamorous parties she frequented in Paris, a fire thrower from Germany who escaped from the circus, and a psychic gypsy who told him he would become the wisest man in Lebanon, just before he laughed her out of the shop.

But little did Matias know that on this day, he was destined to meet the customer that would change the course of his life forever.

Raphael sipped the last drop of his Turkish coffee and took in a deep breath. The scent of expresso hung heavily onto the air. He wanted to remember the sweet smell of the coffee shop before he took off to India. India had a whole other blend of aromas of its own-- a total attack on the senses.

The man was so clearly well-traveled. Even his smirk was cultured. He carried a backpack and a sachet full of books and journals.

"Italian?" Matias asked Raphael, as he cleared the coffee cup from his table.

Raphael scribbled something in his journal and looked up at the barista. "Spanish," he replied. "I'm from Barcelona, but I belong to no country. I've been a traveling nomad for years."

There was a gorgeous twinkle in the nomad's eyes; two diamonds pressed into a tan face. The living portrayal of a Spanish heartthrob in all those romance books many of Matias' customers read, Raphael was so well sculpted it was a wonder how beauty didn't shoot out of him and spill everywhere like water. Matias was slightly intimidated, and thought how easy Raphael's life must have been with looks like that.

"I would love to travel the world like you do," Matias said, "but then I'd have to stop working and then I'd never have enough money to build my villa next door to Monsieur Jumblatt."

"You might find when you have your villa, that you've sacrificed your health and life to get it. And then you'll be too content with the way things are to travel."

"Don't you ever want a home?" Matias asked.

"Maybe one day," Raphael replied, "but I'm not going to sacrifice my health or happiness for it."

As Matias listened in earnest, he leaned in closer and closer until he found himself sitting at the table with the fascinating nomad. And he remembered the dreams of his youth- before adulthood shackled him to logic and responsibility. It wasn't that Matias was unhappy, because in many ways he had many reasons to be joyful, but something was missing- his life lacked truth.

"Every time I went on the road, my heart floated on a cloud of happiness," Raphael explained his reason for traveling, "but when I returned home to my job, I was always disappointed and never knew why."

"I know that feeling," Matias replied, "but I could never just quit my job to travel the world. Excuse me for saying, but that's just something hippies and gypsies do. I have responsibilities."

"I'm neither a hippie or a gypsy," Raphael said, "but I understand your point. Most people are too afraid to do what they truly desire, because if they try, they might fail. If they never try, they'll never fail; and that's easier to deal with. I was one of those people, but taking the leap has changed my life and made me happier."

Matias didn't want to talk about dreams and failures anymore. His only dream right now was to keep working and raise enough money to eventually build a villa next to Jumblatt's.

"My customers are always telling me amazing stories," Matias said. "I bet you've met incredible people on your travels."

"I lived for a month in a Venezuelan Church and worked on a vineyard near the French Alps for six months," Raphael recounted. "I helped build huts in Thailand and traveled across the Amazon, twice."

Raphael became silent for a moment and his reminiscence was now converted into a sweet longing.

"But there's one person and one place that would trump all of those experiences combined," Raphael continued. "The Great Guru in Rishikesh."

"I've heard of that city," Matias said. "In India."

"Yes. It's the birthplace of yoga, and home to the Great Guru."

"What makes him so great?" Matias asked.

"I've heard stories about how he granted people enlightenment in just seconds. He can awaken a person with the wave of his hand. Awaken from the dream. Awaken to reality. Just one tap of his finger upon your brow. How great a guru!"

Raphael was getting louder with excitement. This embarrassed Matias and he looked around to make sure no one was listening. The ancient secretiveness of it all reminded Matias of those theology lessons at his school cathedral. He was like a child again, learning about a holy man who was hidden from the rest of the world, and pining to know more.

"Are you going to see him?" He asked in a whisper.

"Yeah," Raphael said. "There's a cargo ship that leaves from here in Beirut to India tomorrow, and I plan on visiting the great guru. It's a long shot, though. He is notorious for turning students away, and accepts only the most sincere and pure of heart."

"Sounds like a waste of time to me," Matias said cynically. "But I admire your passion and I've enjoyed this conversation. Your coffee is on the house. And please let me give you a croissant for the road."

Matias handed the traveler a chocolate-filled croissant from the display and sent him on his way. Meanwhile from across the cafe, the lazy shop owner watched with greedy eyes.

He was a hard man composed purely of darkness.

But the question was, why?

What made him this way?

For the answer to that question, one had to go back about a decade. The owner used to be a kind and gentle man with a giving spirit. He was blessed with a saintly nature and gave away coffee to the poor during the cold months. That all changed suddenly one day and he became cruel after seeing his dog get struck by a car. The owner kneeled beside his dying pup, held him in his arms and cried. And just before the dog took his last breathe, he licked the tears from his owner's face.

Seeing Matias give away a free croissant, he trembled with anger, and approached Matias.

"Hear my question and don't deny anything," the owner said. "Did that customer pay for the coffee and croissant or did you give it away?"

Matias was afraid. He had never seen the owner like this.

"I gave it to him. You can take it out of my check- It'll never happen again…"

"You stole from me. I can never trust you again, Matias."

It was over.

"I'm sorry, but I can't have you work here anymore. Don't come back tomorrow."

"Four years..." Matias pleaded. "Four years I never asked for more money. I worked harder than anyone else you've brought in..."

"Matias- I've made my decision."

"Please, be kind!"

"Why should I be kind?" The owner said. "What has kindness ever done for me?"

As though the loss of his job was going to kill him, images of his life flashed before his eyes like a lucid dream: climbing fig trees in his childhood home, the death of his cat 'Halo', seeking the approval of his judgmental father, walking through the regal halls of Jumblatt's villa, playing chess with his great uncle. Clingy memories he thought he had forgotten, suddenly sprouted into his mind like roots from the past.

Matias didn't say another word. He just closed his eyes and heard a song of exceeding misfortune. He looked around at the people enjoying the coffees he brewed for them and suddenly they were transformed in his eyes from nagging regulars to dear customers he would never see again.

Four long years he worked at the same coffee shop and it only took him four minutes to lose his job. The fired barista became drunk with bitterness.

He saw the dream of owning his own villa slip away from his grasp. Dreams are the worst thing a person could have, he thought. They bring happiness to a lucky few, but for most they bring only disappointment and make a person resentful. It's better to live without dreams, he thought, to avoid the chance of being disappointed at all. Even the word itself is strange - dreams - it lives in every room, hiding in the dark corners, wearing a cloak of invisibility while shouting at you to find it.

Across the room, a boy about the same age as Matias sat and read his book. He had blonde hair and a face even angels would admire. His clothes were fashionable and the keys to his luxury car hung tauntingly from his finger. Matias watched him for a moment.

"Rich, handsome," Matias muttered to himself. "What have *you* ever had to work for in your life?"

He was beginning to grow more resentful about everything around him. How could I be stupid enough to be generous and careless all at once? Matias said to himself. I could have killed the nomad, slaughtered him dead, and the coffee shop owner would probably have been more willing to let me stay, Matias thought. At least then he wouldn't have lost any money, which is all that heartless man cares about.

Matias was surprised at his own ugly thoughts. He knew it was wrong to think such things, and he decided to leave the store before he became even more bitter.

The jobless youth walked down the ancient streets of his Lebanese town and turned his gaze heavenwards, wondering if there was a vengeful God staring back down, proud of the misfortune He cast upon the boy. Matias was never a God-fearing man, but he thought now about a Biblical verse he heard once. "You who dwell in Lebanon, nested in the cedars, how you will groan when pangs come upon you, pain like a woman in childbirth!" And he wondered if this is the pain they were talking about- a sort of penance that every settler of Lebanon shall be sentenced to endure.

"I'm only going to ask once," Matias prayed silently. "And if You're listening, You'll reveal an answer to me right now. Not when I get home, but right now. That way I'll know it's a sign from You. Show me why this is happening to me, and tell me what I'm supposed to do now. I'm lost. Please, please show me."

Prayers are timeless, and as a sincere person prays, he is aware of their timelessness.

The first thing Matias saw when he looked down was a local bookstore he had passed by hundreds of times during his walks to the shop, but was always in too much of a rush to step inside. He stood at the door, watching people flip through books and he felt a homecoming in his soul. He felt like he was supposed to be there.

Inside, there were rows and rows of books separated into a wide range of categories: photography, philosophy, mathematics, history, religion, and any other topic one would want. Matias didn't know where to start so he just strolled around.

He walked into a section about spirituality and paused when he felt a chill in his spine. A quiver of speech came to his lips: show me.

He felt sort of crazy to believe that he was being guided by something he couldn't even see. He sat down on the ground and rested his face in his hands, unsure of what he was going to do with his life. The sound of a book falling to the floor got his attention and he looked around to see if someone had dropped it, but no one was near him.

He picked up the book, leather-bound and thin in size. The words *"Sat Nam"* were displayed on the cover. Under it, a sentence: *Healing Kundalini Yoga*.

He flipped through it quickly and saw different mantras and illustrations of yoga postures. There were chapter titles like "silencing the ego" and "how to awaken" and "I Bow Before My Higher Self". He stopped at a page which had been previously folded in the top corner, a former reader's footnote. Matias began to read one of the paragraphs in the middle of the page:

Fate is nothing more than self-effort. All things you experience are a result of your own self-effort, whether it be from this lifetime or the last. The circumstances you were born into now, are a direct result of your self effort from a past incarnation. But the present is endlessly more powerful than the past, and if your present intention is stronger than your past self-effort, it will triumph.

His life was missing truth, and he didn't know where to find it, but a feeling inside his heart told him that this book was a start.

Matias shut the book and looked around. He didn't want one of the coffee shop regulars to see him in the spiritual section, let alone carrying a mysterious book. He wouldn't know how to approach the conversation or what to say about a topic he didn't know anything about. Besides, it's a small town where word travels quickly and they would probably ask him why he got fired and what his future plans were- a talk he would be happy to avoid.

Matias walked to the front of the store to pay for the book. He held it low so that no one would recognize the cover. He even grabbed a couple of other "regular" books that he didn't care to read just so that the leather one would blend in more unsuspiciously.

"Just these?" the cashier asked.

She had an unusual beauty with sadness everywhere; sad eyes and a sad smile on a sad face. But in the sadness there was brightness too. A calm intensity which felt simultaneously invasive and welcoming, as though he were peering into the window to her soul, but unable to tell if he was looking in or looking out. Her gaze caught Matias' attention most of all. It was a curious stare, a feeling that she had read a thousand exciting books and that she could compare a man to one of the exciting characters she'd met in a fictional place. Matias was sucked in by her eyes, two black holes, and in them he saw not only stars but the whole universe. She spoke seashells and each word played the ocean to his ears.

"Yes," he replied.

As she sorted them, she paused and held the mysterious one in her hands. Matias was beginning to sweat, he just wanted her to put the book in a bag and leave it alone.

"I've heard a lot of things about this one, but I haven't had a chance to read it. Can you tell me what you think after you're finished with it?" the girl asked.

Matias nodded.

As she rang up the books, he noticed her bracelet, even admired it. It looked like something from another century: two round plaques, one gold and one silver, bound together. Two seemingly opposite elements forged in the fire to become one perfect whole, eternally sealed.

"I've seen you at the coffee shop, you're the barista there," she continued.

Matias was anxious. He just wanted to take his books and leave, but on the other hand he was captivated by the girl. She was different.

"Yeah, the barista, I recognize you," she went on. "You look like everyone else in this town. I bet you even watch the same mindless movies they do so you'll have something to talk to them about. You hear them order the same drinks day in and day out- living their lives robotically. You probably even say things like, 'it's supposed to rain on Monday' and 'I heard a funny joke the other day', but in reality you're just dying to grab them by the shirt and say, 'where do you think we all come from?' and 'is this all just a dream?' I'm like you. I'm not one of *them* either."

As she spoke, Matias watched her rosy lips- he wanted to kiss them. He imagined she was his wife and they were standing in the library of their villa next door to Jumblatt's.

But he didn't say anything. He was too afraid. He bought the books, smiled politely, and never shopped there again.

Matias walked home in a rush. Cliche as it may be after any misfortune has occurred, it actually was a rather windy day. The wind in Lebanon is a prolific storyteller, both ancient and profound. If a breeze blows by and you don't hear the poems of Khalil Gibran, you aren't listening hard enough.

God was fair to the Lebanese; he gave them very little in the realm of natural resources- no oil or coal- (just the Biblical cedars that made them famous), but he gave them *charm*; And charm is the most essential trait to survive in the world- it helps a person glide through life, helps them get up in the morning. The Lebanon Matias knew was philosophically enchanted. But the Lebanon it could have been, had it lived up to the potential Princess Europa and Saint Charbel saw in it, would have been the most revered nation that ever existed. *That* Lebanon was just a borrowed memory now, so old only the wind remembered it.

Lebanon was the tree that sprouted from the seeds of philosophy, even as the Bible declared, "The righteous will flourish like a palm tree, they will grow like a cedar in Lebanon. This town was a fairly small one, like most mountain towns, and it had no street names or signs directing people. If a stranger wanted to find someone's house, they had to ask around and follow directions like "drive up the hill across from the pharmacy and keep driving until you see the yellowstone house on the left." Needless to say trying to deliver packages in a place like that would be a nightmare. So everyone just picked up their mail from the one post office in town. Also like most mountain towns in Lebanon, the city had one dominant religion. In some cities it was Christianity and in others Islam. And everyone was passionate and sure of their religion. This town was predominantly Druze, a small sect found mostly in Lebanon, Syria and Israel. The Druze were modest people and very secretive with their religion, which was more of a philosophy really. They could only marry within the religion and only the sheiks knew its true

Mornings everywhere are beautiful, but they are most beautiful in Lebanon. The punctual sun arrived that day in a fine yellow dress. When Matias woke up, he thought he was late to work and frantically began to throw on his clothes. It was a habit developed over the past four years. It wasn't until he tripped over the mysterious book that he remembered the series of events from the day before.

He picked the book off the floor. Put it on the nightstand. Then off the nightstand and on his pillow, so he would remember to read it at night. Then he realized he was just resisting- putting off the reading until later. But later would never happen. Now. It had to be now.

The first page was all about the importance of living in the present.

"Take this very instant now, and know that this is all there is in eternity. In this present moment, nothing from the past can reach you, and here you are sinless, because your sins are in the past and the past is a dream. From this holy instant, you will go forth with no sense of fear of the future and no sense of being followed by the past."

Matias sat in a meditative pose with his legs crossed and spine straight. He focused on his breathe, rhythmic like the ocean tides. Long inhales through the nose, long exhales through the mouth. It seemed to relax him and he felt like his mind was aligning with his higher self. But after only a minute of bliss, his mind began to wander - his ego - interrupted.

Did I leave the oven on? He thought. *I should call my mom. I can't believe that lazy slob fired me after four years of hard work.*

He recognized how insane his thoughts were- How could he have left the oven on when he hadn't even cooked breakfast yet? Still- he was not in control of what thoughts sprouted from his head.

A walk, that's what I need. To clear my mind, he thought. *And then I'll come back to my meditation.*

Matias walked along the Mediterranean coast. The ocean always had some strange way of calming him no matter what he was going through. It was something about the perfect blend of soothing blue colors, soft feel of the sand, and the peaceful sound of waves that came together to create a symphony of nature. Water is God's tranquilizer, he thought, with the effortless power to sedate man's mind.

The wind blew toward the west and Matias turned his head to the East. A large cargo ship was sitting on the pier. Matias wiped his brow and gazed in wonder at the ship's glory; the sun gleamed against its polished exteriors. The other people walking down the coast marveled at the vessel, mere dwarfs in its vast shadow.

Men were loading the ship with huge boxes while cranes lowered steel crates loaded with goods onto the deck. Matias was so fascinated by the ship that he walked onboard to get a closer look.

A large Arab man grabbed Matias by the shoulder.

"What are you doing on this ship, boy?" he asked. "It's dangerous here."

"I'm sorry, I was just curious..."

"Get out of here, before you get hurt," the man said in a threatening tone that suggested he might do the hurting.

Then, a familiar voice intervened.

"My friend!" It was the nomad from before.

"You!" Matias said.

"You decided to come, huh? Caught the travel bug!"

"Come where? No, no I'm not going anywhere. I got fired- yesterday..."

"Fired?" Raphael asked. "Great! We'll open some champagne and celebrate!"

"Celebrate what? My life is ruined! I was saving money to build a villa, everything was going according to plan and then you came in and I messed up and I don't know what to do."

"Do what I say- celebrate!" Raphael said. He was oblivious to the way 'ordinary' people thought. "Come to India and have an adventure, and worry about your villa later."

"I have to go home, there are things I need to do," Matias replied.

"What do you need to do?" Raphael asked.

"Well, I can't think about it on the top of my head, but there's always stuff."

"Everything happens for a reason," Raphael said. "You're here because you're supposed to be- go with it."

"I don't have any of my stuff," Matias countered.

"We'll get everything we need on the road," Raphael said.

"I can't afford a ticket to India," Matias countered again.

"Pay your way by doing work on the ship, like me," Raphael said. He had an answer for everything.

Matias was scared, but that was all the reason to do it. Anything worth exploring is going to be a little scary. Matias looked to the sky. "Show me" he prayed the day before.

"Find the captain," Raphael suggested. "He's all business, but he has a soft spot. Tell him your circumstances and he'll find a place for you onboard."

Matias walked to the captain's office below the deck. It was in many ways like an abandoned ghost ship:

the lights flickered, the floors creaked with every step he took and droplets of salt water leaked from the ceiling.

There was screaming from behind a door that was cracked open. A man was yelling and cursing about a bloody-something. Matias peeked through the crack in the door and saw the captain talking to a crew member. He expressively waved his hands as he spoke.

"You can navigate through the seven seas, you can catch a hundred fish in three hours, but coffee- a single cup of coffee you can't make!" The captain yelled shaking his fist in the man's face.

A silver expresso machine stood to his right, and although it looked like an antique, it was beautiful and rare and Matias admired its craftsmanship.

The captain kicked the expresso machine. "Find the merchant that sold you this piece of junk and get every penny back, or bring me his pinky!"

"Wait!" Matias exclaimed, quickly regretting his outburst and covering mouth.

Both men turned their attention to the boy intruder.

"And who are you?" the captain asked.

"My name is Matias."

"Trespasser," the captain said to the crew member. "Throw him out."

The man, much larger than Matias, grabbed him and started to drag him out, when Matias yelled "I'm a coffeemaker!"

"Wait," the captain commanded.
Then to Matias … "what?"

"I was a barista in the busiest coffee shop in town," Matias said, still afraid but faking confidence now.

"May I?"

The captain nodded.

"What will you have?" Matias asked.

"Cappuccino," the captain replied. "Light foam."

Finally, a different request, Matias thought.

Matias had never used an antique expresso machine like this one, but all his years as a barista taught him to master the art of brewing the perfect cup. He felt an invisible hand instructing his own to the proper handles and knobs. His hands moved swiftly like the wings of a nightingale. The two steady eyes of the captain stared fixedly at him and he could feel the cold gaze upon him. He was accustomed to the heavy stares of the coffee shop owner, and focused his attention only on the warm, dark coffee as it poured into the cup, filing it to the brim. Next he began to create the foam for the topping. The captain marveled at the boy's mastery of an ancient art.

"Hurry up," the crew member said.

"Don't rush the boy!" The captain snapped back.

Matias added a scoop of foam to the top of the coffee, then picked up a squeeze-bottle of chocolate syrup conveniently placed beside him, and carefully drew the image of a rose into the foam. He handed the porcelain cup to the captain, and when it was received, Matias took one step back. And waited. The night before, he whispered a promise to himself that he would never brew another cup of coffee and today it was the cappuccino he made that would determine the course of his life.

The captain took a short sip. He looked up and puckered and licked his lips. Then he took a second, longer sip.

"This cappuccino was brewed by the same hand that gives a flower its scent," the captain said. "I would be honored to have you onboard if you prepare a cup like this for me every day."

Matias could not help but to smile, and it spread across his face for the first time in a long while. He looked at the crew member who rushed him before and grinned.

He was bound for holy India.

Raphael was most pleased to see his new friend when they met again on deck.

"I have to remind you, there is no guarantee that the Great Guru will see us," Raphael commented.

"In my brief meditation, I heard the song, and now I seek the choir," Matias said. "I have to try."

Matias thought about what people would say when they found out he left the country, abandoning his ancestral home... and his dreams, they would instigate. He was always outspoken about his goals and never hid the fact that he was working toward a villa next door to Jumblatt's. Now the gossip-fueled residents of his little town would say that he fled the country out of shame for not being able to fulfill his dream. But Matias didn't care anymore. Let them talk, he thought. Today was Independence Day, Matias' Day, he was Christopher Columbus out to find his truth. It was a new year with a brand new resolution: discover truth.

The days on board were spent mostly talking about the Great Guru. Raphael was so well-read and full of information about meditation, yogis and saints. The nomad enjoyed repeating all the things he'd learned in books, but Matias mostly nodded and listened, speaking only when he felt like there was something he could add: a life experience, stories he heard from coffee shop guests, or something he learned from the language of coffee, the language only attentive baristas understood.

The other crew mates kept to themselves and did their work. Matias only spoke to one other person onboard aside from Raphael and the captain. She was the daughter of a wealthy shipping tycoon who allowed her to work and travel on his ships after she refused to spend her life on shopping sprees and other excessive luxuries like her two sisters before her.

Matias thought that maybe when a person decides to stop resisting what the universe puts in front of them they become more open, and in that openness, find others who also abandoned resistance to follow their hearts' silent wishes.

Matias felt like he was Columbus, in search of a new world and discovering new parts of his soul along the way. When the whales moaned at night, he felt they were serenading him, and when the wind blew a little harder, he felt like it was whispering a secret to him. As frightening as it all was, he knew in his heart that he was on the right path. One day as he tried once more to meditate beneath the stars, he was summoned by to the captain's office by the big man who tried to throw him out when Matias first arrived on the ship. Matias was afraid. He thought the Captain might be dissatisfied with the way Matias was preparing the coffee. His heart was a racehorse and his palms sweaty. He wiped his hands on his pants and walked as slowly as possible down to the captain's office. The only thing that gave him peace of mind was knowing that there was no way to kick him off the ship. There was nowhere to go, except into the ocean, but surely the captain didn't hate the coffee *that* much.

Matias sat in front of the captain, who was quiet and serious. The captain poured Matias a drink for a change.

"Matias, do you know how I became a wanderer?"

"No, sir."

"When I was your age, I went through the same thing you're experiencing now. I wanted to go to the East and find spirituality, and I was close too. I made it all the way to Tibet, where I lived with a family of monks. We woke up before sunrise every morning and meditated for hours. And then we prepared our own lunch from our own garden. We had no material possessions and devoted every second to a higher calling. But I had something inside of me that I see inside of you: Fear. The kind that lived dormant for a while, but rises out of nowhere and drives you away from your path. You can't let that stop you."

"It is natural to be scared, even as it is natural for a diamond to sparkle" Matias said. "How can I not be?"

"Be scared," the captain replied. "But don't let it deter you. Keep going. It's too late for me in this life, but you can find truth."

The captain walked over to his desk and opened the bottom drawer. He took out a small pouch and placed it in Matias' hand.

"An old sage in India gave me this relic when I was last there," he said. "If I had it when I was younger, things might have turned out differently for me. Better, perhaps."

Matias pulled the relic out of the pouch and inspected it. It was a heavy silver coin with a cross in the center and a tiny image engraved in each corner: A dove, a snake, a lantern, and a sanskrit word that he couldn't read.

"What is it?" He asked.

"If you hold it tight and ask faithfully, the relic will absorb your fears. It won't be permanent, but your fear will disappear. It's served me well many times and I want you to have it now."

"Thank you," Matias said. "I'll carry it close in India."

*

The air changes when you approach India. Aromas of essential oils and colorful spices blend harmoniously with the scent of slums and ashrams. You can smell the poor, see the wealthy, hear the seekers, taste the ancientness and *feel* the enlightened.

Matias made one last cup of cappuccino for the captain, who swore to the heavens he would never drink coffee from another hand again.

Never before had Matias seen so many colors- it was as though India was playing a game where the objective was to see how many colors it could fit into one place. And everywhere around him were shops and people and food.

Raphael ran like a child from one place to the next, jumping around with no particular pattern, just wanting to see everything. Matias chased after him from place to place until they finally ended up in a restaurant that served food to mostly locals. Raphael insisted they have an authentic Indian meal, and Matias was not going to argue with that. After all, the smells were the perfect bait to lure his appetite.

The restaurant had statues of Hindu gods scattered around, mainly of Lord Krishna and Ganesha, the elephant god regarded as a remover of obstacles.

"Pick up the naan bread and fold it like this," Raphael showed Matias. "And then scoop up the masala like you would with a spoon."

Matias had a new favorite cuisine, and he thought of how wonderful it would be to open an Indian restaurant in his hometown. He missed that town, but there was no thinking of that now - he had a mission - to find the Great Guru.

But his comrade was distracted by something stronger than all things strong, the temptation of a beautiful woman.

"I'm going to marry that girl," Raphael said, staring across the street.

Matias turned in the direction of Raphael's gaze, but before he could say anything, Raphael burst out of his chair and ran toward the girl. Matias was beginning to notice that his new friend was a man driven by his impulses.

With the exception of holy men and those with trained minds, man is but a slave to sexual attraction. If the beauty of flesh and muscle were everlasting, then the blinded attraction would be justifiable, but the body does not last very long at all. What was once charming and alluring, becomes feeble and weak- merely a meal for worms beneath the soil. Yet still, a youthful man will lose his wisdom and watch it transform to utter stupidity in the face of physical beauty. The sight of something sexually appealing strengthens his imagination and dumbs his spirit.

Raphael enveloped the girl with questions: he wanted to know her name and her interests and about her hometown, but mostly he just wanted to hear the angel speak.

She told him she knew a place with a river that ran since the start of time and that all lovers who crossed it together were blessed in eternal matrimony by the goddess Shiva herself.

Matias protested with Raphael not to go to the river.

"We came here to see the Great Guru," Matias reminded him. "She can come with us, but we must go."

But the chains of temptation, though made of invisible desire, are hard to break.

"Go to the Great Guru, my eager friend," Raphael replied. "I will meet you in Rishikesh right after this angel and I are blessed in the river."

The two new lovers, infatuated and each more impulsive than the other, ran off hand in hand, leaving the naive Lebanese boy on his own in a strange land that suddenly became less colorful and lot more foreign.

A thought fell into his mind and he remembered the town he left behind, the job he lost and the girl from the bookstore. He wondered what she was doing then, and if maybe she too was thinking of him. They were so far apart now, they might as well be living in different worlds. He wanted to fly to her. Fly over the sea of colors that was India, and fly above the great pyramids of Egypt where the ghost of Cleopatra's cats licked their paws, and he wanted to fly high above Monsieur Jumblatt's villa until he finally got to the bookstore and snatched the girl away so they could fly together above a world that had nothing left to offer them. She asked him to return and tell her about the things he read in the mysterious book, and he felt in his heart that one day he would.

Matias went to the train station, which was filled with even more people in an even smaller place. They resembled speedy ants scrimmaging through the halls of their colony. A cluster of children, five or six in total, surrounded Matias and began to dance around him. Riddled with scars and dressed in shaggy clothing, they looked like beggars.

"I'm sorry, I don't have any money," Matias said.

"No want money," one boy replied. "We make magic for you."

Matias was anxious to go buy his train ticket to Rishikesh, but pity fell into his heart and he reluctantly stayed to watch their little act.

The main boy held a long, long, red silk rope. Long enough, Matias thought silently, to line the entire way to the Great Guru in Rishikesh. He slowly lowered the rope into a basket and instructed Matias to keep his eyes focused on the rope, while the other children danced around him, making it hard for him to concentrate.

Suddenly the kids, on exactly the same beat, picked up and ran so fast into the sea of people that it was impossible to spot them after only a few seconds. Matias was confused, not knowing what was going on. Did something frighten them? Was this part of the trick?

A feeling of unease overcame him and he reached into his back pocket. It was empty. His wallet was gone. Pickpocketers.

Luckily he still had what he saved from the coffee shop back at his home in Lebanon, but he was now penniless in India with no way to get to Rishikesh and no way to return home. He was angry with himself for letting Raphael persuade him to come in the first place. I should have just found another job and continued to save money for my villa, he thought.

He figured that perhaps the train operators would take pity on him and give him a ride to Rishikesh without any charge, but he quickly realized that wasn't going to happen when the ticket salesman, accustomed to tourists being scammed out of their money, laughed him away.

"No money, no ticket," the salesman said.

A group of American yogis, dressed completely in white garments with white beanies and wraps around their heads, heard the conversation between Matias and the ticket salesman. One of them introduced himself as Sat Deva Khalsa.

"You're on your way to Rishikesh," Sat Deva said. "You must be a seeker of truth, like us."

"I was on my way to see the Great Guru..."

"We're headed to the Golden Temple in Amritsar," Sat Deva said. "We'll gladly pay for your ticket to come with us. You can meet other yogis and pilgrims there and prepare yourself to see your guru. You're too tense to go now."

"Thank you, I promise I'll pay you back," Matias said.

"Don't worry about it, we believe in helping those in need. The universe brought you to us."

Matias wasn't sure if he believed in the universe bringing them together, but he smiled, nodded his head and accepted the ticket to Amritsar. On the train, he sat with the friendly yogis, which was only courteous after they paid his way. He never had friends from the west before and was surprised to see how kind they were to him, treating him like an old friend, a member of the group. Being the paranoid youth that he was, witnessing several little wars in Beirut during his short lifetime, he kept his hands ready to guard against attack from the seemingly innocent yogis. He kept saying to himself, "they are going to try something right now. Now. Now." He continued to say it over and over again, to make sure he stayed on his toes.

Matias' hands were clutched in fists and his brow scrunched with stress, creating ridges in his forehead.

"What those children did to you was awful," the oldest of the yogis said. Her voice was soft, but certain and firm- it was frailty paired with strength. "But they're from the slums and don't have many options."

"I know, I know," Matias said. "I know I'm supposed to forgive, but it's so hard. When someone hurts you, how can you just forgive them?"

"By practicing," she replied. "By realizing that they hurt you in the past, but the past is a dream. It only happened in your mind. There's a quick meditation I can teach you to help. It only takes a few minutes to do."

She showed Matias the hands movements, called mudras, and like a mirror he mimicked her. Then she chanted a mantra and controlled her breathe and like an obedient parrot Matias did the same. He visualized the glow of a candle resting between his brows, a tiny sparkle of brilliance that burned away all the negative emotions he held within him. It burned away lifetimes of self doubt, making room in his body for grace to enter and carving out a space where peace could make a home to stay with him always.

When Matias opened his eyes after three minutes, he felt as though he had just come out of the water after being submerged for hours. His mind ignited like a fire and lighted every corner of his consciousness as his cells danced.

"I feel amazing," Matias said. "It's like I undressed myself of anger as simply as I would a jacket."

The wise yogi just smiled. She knew the feeling, and words don't do it justice.

"When someone tempts you to hate them," she said. "Just say to yourself, 'It is not this person's actions I would focus on. I know that my brothers and sisters are one with me' and this will help your mind to forgive."

Matias realized that there was good in all things. Even the darkest moments held slivers of light. There were two pieces of good Matias was able to see in the ordeal at the train station. One was that the children might go a little less hungry now that they had his money, and the second was that he was given the chance to meet other seekers of truth and journey to a place he might never have gone to otherwise. The Golden Temple, he thought, must hold at least some secrets of truth.

Matias didn't know what truth was, but he imagined it had gentle ears that listened to your lies and transformed them into pure light. Nor did he know what truth sounded like, but he thought it must have a motherly voice and soft lips that whispered all the secrets of the universe.

When the group arrived at Amritsar, they saw many other pilgrims there who traveled from all corners of the world to visit the Golden Temple and bathe their feet in its holy waters.

The yogis introduced Matias to an elderly Indian couple who were friends of the temple. They ran a little bed and breakfast for visiting pilgrims and allowed Matias to live in one of their rooms and pay for it by doing domestic work around the Inn.

The place was empty. There were six guest rooms in total and aside from the one Matias lived in, only one other room was being rented.

Matias' room was modest to say the least. It looked like the servant's chamber in a king's palace. Yellow walls, yoga mats, and simple Sanskrit furniture made of wood- Just the essentials: a bed, a nightstand, an armoire for hanging clothes. The good thing, Matias thought, was that the simplicity in decor made it easier for him to clean. He wiped his hand along the windowsill and watched his fingertips turn gray. Gray from the bleakness of a room that hasn't been lived in.

Matias performed his duties with the careful touch a bird gives to building its nest. He wasn't lazy with his chores. His father told him years before that laziness might succeed in the beginning, but it always commits suicide in the end. He dusted the window sills in every room and swept the cold floors until they were clean enough that his own compulsive mother would approve.

The inn keeper and his wife were charitable, and in their charity, never allowed a person to feel indebted. The wife told Matias he could call her 'Ammee' - the Urdu word for mother.

"Ammee," Matias said one day. "The sign outside is old and hard to read. Let me make a better one for you."

"If you feel it is necessary, you have my blessing," she replied.

Matias sat on the floor in front of the Inn's entrance and created a small workspace. He took the old sign, made of wood, and painted it with an attractive shade of paint that he mixed until it became the splendid color of a grapefruit layered with gold.

While the paint dried, he sat in silence with a cup of golden milk, a simple mixture of turmeric and honey in warm milk, and watched devotees walk down the street toward the Golden Temple. Ammee had taught him that breathing only four long breathes a minute puts a person in a meditative state. He paid close attention to his inhales and exhales until he felt he was truly in a walking meditative state.

He took a brush dipped in black paint and wrote the name of the Inn on the board, adding a smaller line underneath: Sat Nam.

Matias fell in love with the sign more and more with each minute it dried in the hot, Indian sun. When it was dry enough to move, he hung it above the Inn's front door and stepped back to admire his handy work.

A yogi dressed in white garments approached the Inn just as Matias was admiring the sign. He dropped his suitcase to the floor rather abruptly.

"What a charming place!" the yogi said. "Do you know if they have any rooms available?" He asked Matias.

Matias smiled, knowing that the universe materialized this guest as approval of his decision to revamp the Inn's welcome sign.

"Yes, I happen to know they have a perfect room for you with a view of the Golden Temple," Matias told the yogi.

Ammee, too, recognized the divinity behind everything.

"Your path brought you here and together we shall walk hand in hand," she said to Matias after checking the new guest into his room with the scenic view.

After napping in his modest bedroom, Matias woke up at four o'clock in the morning to do what it was he came to Amritsar to do. He had been anticipating his visit to the Golden Temple at the sacred hour when pilgrims and yogis go to find freedom and truth; freedom from illusions and truth of reality.

The temple, in the darkness before sunrise, was bright with magnificence, unblemished by corruptibility. It stood in the middle of a manmade body of water. Around the water was a small wall that lined the entire temple, where seekers of truth swept the surface with straw brooms.

Matias wore his finest white clothes, which is saying a lot, because he really had very limited wardrobe options to choose from. Cleaning the steps, he felt like he and the other pilgrims were doing something grand, like they were saving the world in some small way. Like they were doing something really important. Like they were making waves somewhere on the other side of the planet. Nearby, kids were playing in the trash, competing on who could find the greatest treasures, occasionally carrying something shiny in their hands, waving it in the air to show off to their friends. They were dressed in their dirtiest dumpster-diving clothes, which also isn't saying much because they don't have any nice clothes, really. They were filthy. They were beautiful.

Matias was given a broom to sweep the floor with the rest of the yogis. An old Indian woman walked along the wall in front of him and poured buckets of water onto the marble as he swept it clean. With every sweep, he was told, he was sweeping away his past karma, clearing himself like an artist cleans the old paint from his brushes beneath running water.

Matias felt his karma burning away, and he focused his full attention for the first time in years, on God.

"Creator," he whispered, "I am your creation."

There was no answer, but Matias felt again that he was exactly where he was supposed to be. He wasn't thinking about anything aside from the present moment: sweep left, sweep right, left, right, left, right. And like a bolt of lightning to his awareness, he understood that the past was gone and the future imagined. Everything he wanted or could ever need was right there in that austere moment. Everything else: Raphael, Jumblatt, his villa- were illusions. He felt fully happy. He floated in a stream of laughter, though no one was actually laughing. It was just the energy of joy. The energy of a heart that was learning to laugh again.

The sun began to shine and the yogis descended back to their homes and ashrams. Matias sat outside of the Inn where Ammee and her husband were already awake and cooking breakfast.

He looked upon the world with a new awareness, feeling the pain in the old dog's legs as it stumbled down the road, and sensing the couple's happiness as they embraced in a hug. But none of them noticed him, in this monumental moment, the spiritual climax of his life thus far.

As Matias sat and watched the villagers carry on with their daily routine, he noticed the sun's indiscriminate luminance. The poor beggar and the wealthy tourist walking down the road both felt the same warmth. The sun didn't light one naked face more than another. It dawned on Matias in that moment, that everyone was a small part of God- and to think a person can be separate from God is to think heat is separable from the sun. He realized that the one source was not split into many, as it often time seems. Just as when the flame of a single candle is used to light many candles, it is that same flame that burns all the candles.

As he contemplated this new yet ancient idea, a familiar face smiled at Matias and took a seat beside the boy.

"What are you thinking about?" Sat Deva asked.

"I was just watching the people here," Matias replied. "They're different from people anywhere else, but also the same."

"You seem much happier than when we first met," Sat Deva noticed.

"I feel happier," Matias said. "I can't stop smiling."

"That's the power of meditation. But I sense that something still bothers you."

Matias was holding on to a seed of guilt from his past and he felt its weight now more than ever. Now that he was away from his family and his country.

"My parents could have had a big house. They could have spent their old age taking trips to exotic countries, but instead they spent all their money making sure I had the best upbringing. I went to the best schools and always had everything I needed."

"That sounds beautiful," Sat Deva said. "Why does this thought burden you?"

"Because I could have helped them," Matias said. "I made enough money at the coffee shop to send them on a trip or make their lives a little easier, but I selfishly hoarded it so that I could one day have my villa next to Monsieur Jumblatt's."

Sat Deva looked at the boy with the cedar-green eyes and saw sadness paired with hope, a nightingale waiting to be freed from his cage.

"Guilt has no place in the mind of a son of Divine Mother, and we are all her sons," he said. "Forgive yourself."

"But what if God won't forgive me?" Matias asked.

"God does not forgive," Sat Deva replied.

Matias felt the sharp sting of those words, but Sat Deva continued:

"God does not forgive, because he doesn't condemn his son in the first place. There is nothing to forgive. Every 'sin' you committed happened only in your mind, not in reality."

"But how can I be *completely* guiltless?" Matias asked.

"You aren't without guilt in time, but you are certainly guiltless in eternity. You say you have sinned, and we all have in the past- but there is no past."

"So my guilt is only in my mind?" Matias asked.

"Everything that happened, you created. They're only thoughts and thoughts can be changed. Matias, The present moment is wildly more powerful than the past. So in this moment, release the past and focus your efforts on what you now want. If your present thoughts and actions are stronger than the ones in the past, they will overcome them and become your new reality."

Sat Deva unlinked the long necklace that hung around his neck and handed it to Matias. It was a brown leather cord with a medallion hanging from the end. Matias recognized the Sankrit symbol, Sat Nam.

"Whenever you forget the truth about yourself and how guiltless you are, look at this necklace and remember that the truth is already inside you."

Matias thanked the yogi for the gift and more importantly, for the reminder of his truth.

"I'm sure we'll see each other again," Sat Deva said, "if not in this lifetime, then another."

"Are you going somewhere?" Matias asked.

"My friends are I are going back to the states," he said. "I wish we could stay longer, but we'll be back next year."

"I owe so much to you," Matias said. "Thank you for bringing me to Amritsar and teaching me about meditation and truth."

The two parted ways, but remained forever linked.
Inside the Inn, Matias looked at his reflection in a mirror in his bedroom. Time has a clever way of adjusting people to their environment and after one month of living at

the Inn, Matias began to look more like a yogi and less like an ambitious youth from the Lebanese mountains. His formally clean-shaved face now dawned a short beard, and he wore the medallion necklace from Sat Deva around his neck. Still, the boy started to see that the reflection was not him, but only an image his mind created. He wasn't the reflection, he was the mirror. And this he knew to be true: that everyone was the seer, the sight, and the seen. Everything was part of one collective consciousness.

For the first time in weeks, Matias thought about the Great Guru. By now he had raised enough money from doing chores around the house to take the train to Rishikesh, but he felt bad for leaving Ammee. In many ways he was in a prison, but he loved his prison. He had learned a great deal about himself and the human spirit while living at the inn, but he was on a search for truth, and he wasn't going to find that there. For the type of truth he sought, he needed to find the Great Guru.

He wanted to do something more for Ammee before he could be content with leaving her.

"I think more people will come if we turn the space outside the Inn into a seating area where tired and thirsty yogis can sit with one another," Matias suggested once.

"If you think it's necessary," Ammee replied, "you have my blessing."

Matias was familiar with many of the locals by now, and they with him, and the carpenter across from the inn was more than happy to supply him with scraps of wood to build chairs and tables. Matias had never built chairs or tables before, but his childhood imagination was reborn and he started to put them together like toys. Each one was different. Unique.

Next to the front door, he placed a water cooler with paper cups, where yogis could stop for a drink of refreshing water.

Within one week, yogis began to hang around the Inn on their way to and from the Golden Temple. In two weeks time, every room in the Inn was booked.

"I'm sorry," Ammee told a yogi visiting from Germany. "There are no rooms available tonight."

Matias was pleased at their rise in occupancy since his arrival, but sad to know also that it was time for him to continue on his journey.

"There is one available room, Ammee," he interrupted.

She knew what he was thinking, and nodded sorrowfully.

When the German guest was settled in Matias' former room, Ammee sat with Matias in the seating area outside. She handed him an envelope, filled with money.

"For every guest we've had, I saved a portion for you," Ammee said.

"I can't accept this," Matias said. "You've been so good to have me in your home for this long..."

"None of this money would be here if you hadn't given of yourself to create the sign above our door or the tables and chairs for yogis to enjoy," Ammee replied. "You have been like a son, now let me be like a mother."

Matias bowed his head before the angelic host and took the envelope from her hands, kissing them humbly.

*

The town of Rishikesh has no other purpose than to seek truth, no reality outside of yoga. And all this was apparent from the instant Matias arrived in the holy city. He walked down a long bridge and besought a large statue of Lord Shiva sitting in a perfect cross-legged posture atop the clear waters.

On shore, a class of yogis were positioned in twisted contortion, illustrating both the strength of man's body and the discipline of his mind. He was a foreigner but that didn't matter. Most everyone was a foreigner in Rishikesh; migrant yogis from around the globe seeking something they couldn't seem to find at home. Some stayed for days, others for weeks and months, and a rather dedicated few stayed in the holy place for years. Matias had not the slightest idea how long he would be there, nor what he would find. Uncertainty like that can be maddening.

At first the boy decided he would look for the guru himself, thinking he must live in one of those strange caves or holes in the mountains. But it didn't take long for him to realize he was tired from all the traveling.

Matias turned his head in every direction, seeking a person who looked like they might know where he could find the Great Guru. Everyone had the glazed look of being hypnotized: blissful smiles, slow-moving, calm.

An older man with a long, gray beard and luxurious curls stopped Matias and looked at him with exceeding tenderness.

"I once came across a lost boy in New Delhi," the man said. "He was looking for his mother after they got separated by the crowds of people. Although you don't bear the tears he was shedding, you still remind me of him. Who have you lost?"

"I lost my traveling companion," Matias replied. "But it's who he was supposed to take me to that I seek now. Have you heard of the Great Guru?"

"Yes, of course," the man said. "He's inside of you. There is a great guru in everyone. Awaken that guru through meditation."

Matias was not interested in riddles and philosophy today. He was in search of the guru he believed would teach him wisdom and God-realization.

The old man pointed him in the general direction and as Matias approached the home of the sainted guru, he had fear in his heart. He thought it might be possible it would turn out to be a haunted place- not a haunted house he had actually ever seen, but one that lived in his imagination where spirits roamed freely and chants woke the dead.

He dismissed those thoughts, though, when he suddenly felt the brilliant aura upon reaching his destination, in the bosom of the spacious foothills of the Himalayas.

It was very much like the foothills of Lebanon, but at the same time nothing like them. The people here had an unshakable strength, free of fear and guided by their higher selves. Whereas the people in his village were guided by the superficiality of their egos- strong and united among themselves, but weak and divided among the Western world.

Meanwhile the guru was already outside in his garden when Matias arrived. He had been meditating before, when he heard his higher self whisper something about a future disciple approaching the house. The guru trusted his higher self, but was hesitant to take on a new student, so many of them had become disappointments, abandoning their practice for material pursuits.

"I'm here to see the great guru," Matias explained.

Matias looked upon the face of the master and knew he was in the right place. The guru's face was illuminated by pure light. He was an old man, but he was beautiful to look at, embodying both feminine and masculine energies. It's like he was not man nor woman, simply a whole being.

"I've seen your face in my meditation," the great guru replied. "What is your name?"

"Matias."

"And have you not heard that a guru lives in everyone?" The guru challenged. "What need have you for a guru?"

"I need a guru, because I know nothing," Matias said. "I don't know how to meditate or what to study…"

"I don't accept students anymore," the great guru said rather coldly. "Go back home and be your own guru."

Matias thought of home. There was nothing there for him anymore, except for the girl from the bookstore. The image of her hastily leapt into the center of his mind from wherever it was hiding. For the most part, he forgot that it was even there- he thought the memory was dead, buried beneath a pile of thoughts and dust. It was a plant, lingering in the soil of his mind, waiting to sprout at the slightest drop of water. And then out of nowhere, it leaped back into his awareness- the girl with the sad eyes- standing before him like a painting.

The idea of returning there after enduring travel on a cargo ship, losing his friend and getting his money stolen, was a bleak reality.

Matias poured his body and his heart onto the guru's feet, caressing them the way a queen caresses her fur coats.

"Great guru," Matias pleaded. "I would sooner die than leave here without you as my teacher."

"Then die," the guru said bluntly.

"What?"

The guru held out a dagger in his hand.

"Take this dagger and plunge it into your heart to prove your devotion to me."

Matias was in tears, but he was devoted and meant what he said before. He took the dagger from the guru's hand and thrusted it into his chest it without hesitation. The great guru had tested the boy and demonstrated his magnificent powers over the material world for the first time. Just before the blade reached Matias' chest, it became limp and spilled no blood and caused no bodily harm.

Matias fell again to the feet of the great guru, whose head remained high in majesty above the world, and then he spoke with a bold voice that struck like thunder.

"Rise now, my student."

Every word was an earthquake in the sky.

Matias rose to his feet.

"I will be your guru, because you have acknowledged that you don't know anything and the only way to gain enlightenment is to acknowledge that you know nothing. Truth cannot enter where there are blocks to mar its welcome. You are ignorant of divine truth. But you are humble in your ignorance, and that makes the best kind of student."

"You words are potent," Matias replied. "I would breathe them."

"Then we will begin immediately," the guru said. "I interrupted my meditation to greet you. So we will finish the meditation together."

Matias' stomach, in hunger, cried out for food.

"Is there any chance that we can eat first and then meditate?" He asked. "It's not that I'm ungrateful, but I'm starving."

"You traveled a long way, and must be famished," the guru replied. "But matters of spirit can never be postponed for matters of the body. We will meditate first."

"What if I die from hunger?" Matias asked.

"Then die," the guru said again.

His disregard for life was shocking to Matias, who came from Lebanon, where a history of wars had taught him the importance of survival. But he knew the guru would not let him die, just as he did not let the dagger pierce his heart. It was just a lesson in priorities.

"Don't let your hunger rule over you, for all good gifts from the universe trickle in through self control," the Great Guru said. "There is no level of evil or pain that cannot be dispelled through self control. It's easy to indulge in food, sex and other worldly pleasures, anyone can do that. But it takes true strength to choose to meditate regularly and study spiritual texts. Those are the things that will bring happiness to the heart, and as a result of your self control, all people, even your enemies, will find themselves spontaneously trusting of you."

They walked into the guru's home. The master's bare feet made no sound, while Matias' bulky shoes slapped loudly against the wooden floor with every step. He was a seeker of truth, but clearly needed to learn grace as well.

The main area of the home was a large open space with wooden floors and plain white walls. Simplicity was king there. The only light came from the bright sunshine coming in through several ceiling openings and large windows in every corner.

"The memory of God enters a soundless mind," The guru said. "Be silent, and remember."

Together, student and master meditated with one another for the first time, and the steady divinity of the guru resonated with Matias, allowing him to meditate with a clear mind. The guru had the ability to alter a person's thoughts to allow no negativity to enter, calling the soul's innocence out from its hiding place. They were in the same house, under the same roof, yet worlds apart.

"You are not yet awake, but you can learn to awaken from this dream and see the real world," the guru said. "All that is required of you is a readiness to perceive nothing else."

"But how?" Matias asked.

"By noticing that your hatred is in your mind and not outside of you," the guru replied. "It's the only way to get rid of hatred, and you must get rid of it before you can see the wholly perfect world as it really is."

The boy knew that meditation could help him go inward and get rid of the hatred within him, but he didn't know how to begin. He found it difficult to master the seemingly complicated technique.

"Master," Matias began, "I want to meditate, but I don't know what to do with my hands and how to sit and what to chant."

"Don't be so consumed by the technique," The guru replied. "I find that those from outside India always want to understand the science behind meditation and desperately want to make sure the hands and posture are the 'right' way. As long as your intention is sincere, you will have an enlightening experience."

"I was so frustrated with getting it right the first time I tried to meditate in my bedroom," Matias said. "I'll try to be mindful of my intention this time."

"Don't worry so much about technique," the guru said, "but if you need something to focus on, just watch your breathing. But let your mind be still- don't think about the breathing or add your commentary to it, because that is your ego wanting to judge and makes sense of everything. Simply observe that you are breathing in and observe that you are breathing out- the real you is the observer, not the doer. Just sit still and remain quiet until your heart is a little more open to receive your divine inheritance, that is the point of meditation."

The guru explained that controlling the breathe is the most important thing in life, because when a person learns to control their breathe, they learn to control the dream that is life.

With that thought, they sat in meditative silence and Matias' consciousness rose from darkness while his body clung lovingly to the earth where he sat in cross-legged posture. He was still as a lotus balanced atop a waveless pond.

At first thoughts came and went, and he observed them just like he would observe fish swimming in a tank. When one passed, another swam by. Eventually he stopped watching them at all, and they became fewer and fewer until no more thoughts arose at all.

It seemed like only ten minutes had passed when the guru ended the meditation.

"But master," Matias exclaimed. "How can I find truth with such short meditations?"

"Two hours we've been sitting in quiet," the guru replied. "I thought you might want to eat now."

Two hours felt like ten minutes. That was the power of meditation- its ability to make both mind and time still. His forehead, or third eye as his guru called it, was pulsating. He sat for a moment to take in the feeling and basque in the aura he created, before going into the kitchen to help his guru prepare their dinner.

There was silence and mystery in the guru. The two didn't talk or even look at one another as they ate their simple meal of mung beans and rice with a side of mango and almonds. The higher self is quiet, the ego is talkative. Matias heard only the winged song of bliss as it sat lightly on his shoulder. And the song sounded something like *Sat Nam*.

"How did you become known as a great guru?" Matias asked.

"Oh Matias," the guru replied. "When you overcome the repetitive cycle of death and re-birth called samsara, you too will live here on earth even like Brahma or God Himself."

"Great master, how do I do that?" Matias asked.

"Through meditation, spiritual scriptures, and self-effort," the guru said. "I will show you."

After dinner, the guru handed Matias a large brown sack and told him to put his clothes and shoes inside.

"Going forward you will only wear this," the guru said.

He handed Matias a pair of white silk pants, a white shirt and sandals.

"Just the one pair?" Matias asked.

"When it gets dirty you may wash it," the guru replied. "When you become less attached to material things, you can have more clothes, but they will always be white."

Dressed in his garments of white and seeing things with clearer vision, Matias prepared himself for sleep. And as he did, he felt his old self begin to seep through his zen exterior. He felt that emotion again, fear; and his mind was already wandering, questioning what he was doing in India. This is why I must meditate regularly, he thought. It's so easy to slip back into old patterns and thoughts.

When morning came, it brought with it a sun that absorbed the emptiness. And the sun which absorbed emptiness, brought with it a hunger in Matias. Meanwhile in the kitchen, the Great Guru had already been awake for hours. He allowed Matias to eat and then gave him two bags of basmati rice: one filled with white grains and the other black.

"Since you missed a session with me this morning, I'll show you other ways to meditate in waking life," the guru said. "Everything you do can be meditation if you are mindful."

The guru poured out the two bags of rice, blending together a sea of white and black grains onto the cold floor.

"Separate the rice by color," the guru instructed. "Be mindful of the present moment."

It was a tedious task, and after a while his eyes began to cross and he felt like a man who drives through the never-changing dessert for days. Hours passed. As

Matias sorted the rice, he was focused completely on the present moment. He saw in the rice, joy - joy carried by those tiny brilliances created to sprout from the fields.

Matias broke from his in-the-moment hypnosis when he looked down and saw that he had two neat piles of rice, entirely sorted by color. Hours had passed and he walked around the house in search of his guru, but found that he was alone.

The boy decided to sit outside in nature for a moment and reflect on his conscience state. Rishikesh had so many beautiful views to offer, but still nothing compared to the mountains and coastline of his country. And as he thought of Lebanon, he thought also of its unblemished waters and majestic cedars. He wondered if he would ever return, and something in his heart said yes. It was the same part of his heart that was remembering the girl from the bookstore.

With his eyes closed, he fell into a deep meditation. It was easier now for him to silence the outside world and reach the depths of his mind. It was a black hole, and his spirit a river. He chose to run like the river, rather than consume like the black hole. He saw in his mind, a door. He knew paradise laid behind the door, but he lost the key, or misplaced it, and through meditation he would unlock its promise of truth and bliss.

He heard a creaking sound, like old wooden floors that squeak and groan like an old man with aching joints as you walk over them. His heart lit with joy, thinking maybe the door was finally opening. Oh how glorious awakening will be!

But no. The sound wasn't coming from within. It came from the outside world, waking life, and he opened his eyes to see what intruder disrupted his meditation when he was so close to awakening. Matias saw with his waking eyes, that a tiger had snuck into the backyard where he sat. It hadn't seen him yet, but there was no place for him to go. And instantly that dark emotion came rushing back again: fear.

The she-devil looked directly into Matias' eyes as though the fear was calling out to her, ringing the welcome bell. He tried to control his breath, but he was panicking. He had never seen a real tiger before in his life. He stayed still as a board. No, that's what you do when you see a snake, he thought. He looked around for his master, but the guru was nowhere to be seen. Matias felt death beckon him to his alter.

A part of him was thrilled at the same time. He always held a secret desire to be struck by disaster. Anything that could put a dent in the smooth armor of his life and shatter the polished surface into something more exciting: surviving a groundbreaking earthquake, escaping from a raging fire, dancing beneath a meteor shower, encountering a deadly beast.

The tiger teased him by turning her head away to drink water from a fountain. The boy was like a mouse trapped in a snake's tank, where being eaten alive was the unfortunate inevitable. He leaned against the tree beneath which he was meditating before, and a thought fell into his mind that he could climb as high as he could and hope the tiger would get bored and leave.

But tigers don't get bored. The giant cat veiled her face with a murderous smile.

"She's going to kill me, what bad luck I have," Matias whispered.

And the tiger purred, "The misfortune of one is good fortune for another."

Taking it's purring as a bad omen, Matias climbed the tree as fast as he could. All the baby cedars he climbed in the Lebanese mountains when he was a youth finally came to good use. He wished only his mom could see how all the time 'wasted' didn't go to waste at all. He sat on the first thick branch, but the tiger just laughed under her breathe. 'Man is but meat for jungle cats' she purred.

And as she clawed at the tree trunk, Matias climbed even further- so high, that he sat on the highest branch of the tree. With three swift leaps, using her claws to lift her weight, the tiger pounced onto the first branch where Matias sat before. She would have ended his life had he not continued to climb up further.

Matias gripped the wood branch with a fearful clench and felt its nurturing touch comfort him like a mother assuring safety to her baby. But the air was not as kind. It carried the stench of death and filled his nostrils until he was sick enough to lose his senses. He heard the sound of the tiger gnawing on a branch and he touched his neck, wondering how badly it might hurt when the tiger would dig it's teeth into him and puncture his throat.

Matias was scared, and he was mad at himself for being scared. He spent all this time meditating and learning how to control his emotions and releasing fear of death, only for it to return as soon as he felt threatened.

The guru's thunderous voice declared his arrival, and Matias looked down to see his master's face staring up.

"I leave you alone and you end up in a tree, afraid for your life?" The guru said.

"Master!" Matias said. "Why isn't the tiger climbing down the tree to attack you?"

"Because I am not afraid of the tiger," he replied. "I understand that we are one, so she does not see me as food."

"How can I do the same?"

"When you meet anyone, it is a holy encounter. Practice this thought with everything, even an animal, until it becomes part of your nature. Look at the tiger, and as you see her, you will see yourself. This is your chance at salvation. Give the tiger her place in heaven and you will have yours."

Matias tried to understand, and his guru continued:

"If you overcome your fear, I'll see you tonight for dinner. If you let fear consume you, the tiger will be well-fed today."

The guru left the boy alone. Matias was frustrated and confused, but he thought about something the guru said: 'the tiger will be well-fed." And the boy suddenly knew in his heart that the tiger was just hungry. How could he be angry with her for being hungry? And maybe she had starving baby cubs waiting for her to feed them. As he started to relate to her, he began to feel one with her. He was the tiger and he was the tree branches separating them.

"Come my hungry friend," Matias said. "Come now, let me be your host and you my welcome guest."

Matias was truly unafraid now, and with a voice that no longer shivered, he continued:

"Let me rest in your belly and feed your children, and from my remains feed the soil that flowers may sprout again. My spirit is free like the northern winds and will descend to heaven like a column of light or be born again as a newborn baby, hopefully in a home close to my guru."

In the same instance that Matias *truly* abandoned his fear and heard the music of eternity, the tiger leaped to the ground and ran off. Matias said that he released fear before, but saying the words meant nothing, meaning them meant everything.

Matias descended down the tree slowly, surprised that he was able to climb it so quickly the first time, when he was fueled by adrenaline and the desire to live. He was never more content than in that moment, conquering the ego and unwrapping fear from his mind.

The boy went into the home and saw that the guru was serving tea to a strange man. Matias had never seen him around town before. He was in his mid-40s with the perfect posture of a Roman statue. His wrists were covered with gold bracelets and an enormous diamond hung from a chain around his neck. The gem was more magnificent than any stone Matias had ever seen.

"I'm happy to see you liberated your mind from fear of death," the guru said.

"How did you know?" Matias asked.

"Assume I know everything," the guru responded. Then he pointed to the guest with his eyes. "This kind jeweler will stay with us as he passes through town."

"Nice to meet you, sir," Matias said to the stranger.

"Nice to meet you," the stranger said. "I was told the guru always houses travelers who need a place to stay, so I came to ask for shelter. But I also heard that he doesn't take students anymore, yet here you are. You must be special."

Matias was humbled at the reminder of being a rare exception to his master's refusal to take on new students.

"I am special if I have only a fraction of my guru's wisdom," Matias replied. Although he wore a veil of Zen upon his face, the guru was pleased, and smiled from within.

"To be honest, I respect your devotion, but personally I am a man of logic," the jeweler said. "Enlightenment is for another world. In this world there is only money and power."

"I think following a path of spirituality is the most logical thing in the world," Matias argued.

The guru didn't say a word, just listened.

"Don't get me wrong, I think the world needs spiritual thinkers," the jeweler said. "But you see, my treasure is real. You can see it, you can touch it. I buy things with it- cars, clothes, luxury- and sometimes it buys me people too."

"But none of those things are real," Matias said. "It's like my mom used to tell me- you can't take them with you when you die. And if they were real..."

There was a knock on the door before Matias could finish his thought. He looked at the jeweler with an expression that said 'we'll finish this talk later' and then answered the door. A tall, strong man let himself in and introduced himself as the police chief. The jeweler came rushing over as though he were expecting the guest and took the man's hand.

"Sir, thank you for coming last minute, I assure you it's urgent." He turned to Matias, "might we have some privacy?"

Matias nodded and walked out of the room, but where he sat with his guru in the room next door, they could hear every word clearly.

The jeweler was clearly frightened, stammering his words and speaking like a child who begs for help. "I think the King of Thieves has followed me here. He's after my priceless diamond." The jeweler wrapped his hand around the rare gem, which still hung from his neck. "It once belong to Cleopatra herself, and he will do anything to get it. That's why I came to this ashram, where he will never think to look for me."

"And what exactly can I do for you, sir?" The police chief asked.

"The king of Thieves once stole the crown right off the head of the queen of Jordan. He's the best there is- the most clever thief. I would feel much safer if you could assign officers to guard the ashram just for tonight."

"You are from out of town, and my obligation is to the people who live here. This is not my problem," the police chief responded rather bluntly. "I'm sorry that the King of Thieves has followed you here, but it does not affect my life in any way."

The police chief was a cold man by nature. He left without a hello or goodbye to the great guru and quite frankly was all too concerned with his own needs. The jeweler had a look of defeat on his face and he kneeled before the guru's feet, begging for help.

"Enlightened one, if I stay in Rishikesh tonight, the King of Thieves will steal my diamond and I will lose my most prized possession."

The guru knew that material wealth was nothing compared to the eternal wealth of spiritual gains, but he didn't say that. He never taught by preaching to the world, but simply by demonstrating in quiet recognition that all things are blessed along with him.

"Stay here tonight," the great guru said. "Your diamond is safe."

The jeweler delighted upon hearing the guru's assurance and he praised God in every language he knew. He went to sleep in the room Matias prepared for him, and clutched the diamond around his neck with a strong grip. And when he woke up the next morning, he was still clutching the diamond.

The jeweler hopped out of bed and ran to the living room like a child on Christmas, jumping up and down, "great guru, how great a guru!"

He was shocked to see that the guru was in the living room talking to none other than the very police chief who denied him protection the night before.

"Great guru," the police chief implored, "all the gold was stolen from my safe last night. I beg you to help me retrieve it."

"Why sir," the guru replied, "just yesterday you stood in this very spot and told our guest that the King of Thieves was his problem and not yours. If you had helped capture the thief on behalf of our guest, your treasure would still be with you now. Remember, we are all connected. His problems are your problems, just as your problems are mine. You will not learn to awaken until you learn to awaken your brother. You will not receive compassion or protection until you learn to give it away."

The cold police chief suddenly became a beggar and pleaded for forgiveness and mercy from the great guru.

'In three days your gold will turn up," the guru relented. "Donate one-fourth of it to charity. If you don't, you will lose it all again."

The police chief and jeweler both thanked the great guru continuously and then departed their separate ways. And it was a great surprise to Matias when in three days, he received a letter from the police chief with a piece of pure gold, thanking him and the guru for their kindness, and for returning his gold miraculously. The guru would not accept the gift, but gladly gave it to Matias, telling him he would need it to return home one day. In his bedroom, Matias reflected upon the lessons that the guru was teaching him simply in everyday life.

For the first time since he arrived at the home of the great guru, he thought about his friend Raphael and wondered what the spontaneous nomad was doing. He wondered also if he would ever find his way to Rishikesh. It reminded him of a parable his father told him about a sheik who searched endlessly for God, under one condition: don't ever find Him. Every so often, the sheik came close to finding God, but something would happen and the truth would escape from his grasp. Eventually, the search for God itself became so enchanting and mysterious and sweet, that it consumed the sheik entirely. So one day, when he finally saw the image of God standing before him during a stroll in the mountains, he suddenly realized that his search was over, and it scared him. The search for God was all he dedicated his life to for years, and if he found Him, he wouldn't know what to do with the rest of his life. So he ran like a rabbit running from a lion. He ran away from the image of God and kept on running. Now he continues his search for God, enjoying the pilgrimage, but always careful to avoid the spot in the mountains where he saw Him. This, Matias thought, was also Raphael's journey- he enjoyed the search for awakening but was afraid of actually finding it.

The guru entered Matias' room with a smile on his face. Although Matias felt as though he knew his guru well by now, there was a mysterious inner life in the master, and somewhere in the hallways of his personality there was a stairway leading to an attic that Matias would never enter. It had no key, no way in, and it remained maddeningly unknowable to him, because no map in the entire universe knew the way to enter.

"In my meditation this morning, I heard the name of your soul," he said. "Your soul name is Navtej Singh."

"What's a soul name?" Matias asked.

"It's the vibration of your higher self," the guru replied. "You have been blessed to live as Navtej Singh. For now, continue to be Matias, but know that your soul has a different name."

"Thank you, master." Matias replied. "What does the name mean?"

"Nav is new, and Tej means God's glory and radiance," the guru answered. "Singh is the name all men are given. It means the lion of God, and the power to walk with His grace and courage."

"What is the name for?" Matias asked.

"When you hear the name, or meditate on it, you will expand your consciousness and align with your higher self. The more you hear it, the more the sound current penetrates your surface and brings you into harmony with your destiny."

Their brief conversation was interrupted by the sound of a knock on the door. The knock itself screamed of pain and franticness. The guru opened the door and a mother ran into the home without an invitation inside. She had her infant son, maybe 5-years-old, in her arms and she was pacing back and forth like a lion in heat. Her messy hair and raggedy clothing implied that she was either poor or too occupied with something to take care of herself.

"Great Guru, you must help me!" The woman said. "My son is ill and so close to death, and the doctors tell me they don't know what is wrong with him. I can't afford to take him to the hospital and I feel his breathe is getting weaker by the hour!"

She spoke fast and the words poured out of her so quickly that it took a lot of effort to understand what she was saying. She was like a musician playing the song of desperation with an out-of-tune instrument. Drawn to the mother's cries, Death silently descended upon the ashram and peeked inside through the window. He knew not to enter the home of the Great Guru uninvited.

The guru touched the sleeping boy's forehead and the child opened his hallow eyes, revealing considerable frailty. His complexion was a sickly yellow and his face expressionless.

The woman sobbed bitterly and though agony absorbed her heart, she was able to move her lips and mutter a few more words.

"You can have everything I own," the mother continued. "It isn't much, but my family heirlooms are of some worth. Please! My son has a full life to live and affairs to attend to. Do not neglect him."

The guru was seemingly unaffected by the influences of the outside world, just as mercury is unchanged when thrown into the fire. He stroked her anguished face and calmness fell upon her. Fear was still present, but her shaking was nearly gone and her forehead was no longer scrunched.

"I will heal him," the guru said. "Your son lives."

"Thank you, master, thank you." the devotee said.

The guru took the boy from her arms and laid him gently on a lounge chair with a pillow beneath his head.

Outside, Death murmured, "It looks as though I will not take this one with me today," and he returned to wherever he came from.

The guru knelt beside the ill child and whispered into his ear: "Do not side with sickness, sweet child of God. To believe that you can be sick, is to believe that God himself can be ill." Then he turned to Matias, who had been watching silently thus far, and gave him instructions: "Go into town and bring me a bundle of sage and a cup of turmeric."

In the marketplace, Matias walked down the pathway where vendors lined both sides of the narrow street. One merchant had baskets of rice; there must have been a dozen different varieties: from white and brown to red. The contrasting colors of rice looked so beautiful beside each other. On a shelf above, he sold green and black Mediterranean olives in small glass jars.

Another merchant was selling beautiful silks pillow

covers with images of Hindu deities on them. The rest of the products in the marketplace were equally impressive. There was a shoemaker and a toymaker, a baker and an artist: but Matias was specifically there for two things, sage and turmeric, and as far as he knew, a little boy's life depended on them.

Matias found a vendor with a kind face. She was a Western yogi with blonde hair and blue eyes and a radiant smile that seemed to bless the world. She sold all kinds of things from incense sticks and Hindu figurines to oils and spices.

"Do you have any turmeric and a bundle of sage?" Matias asked.

"Yes, of course," the woman said.

She took a glass jar off the shelf and filled it to the brim with bright yellow turmeric powder and then grabbed a bundle of sage, tied together with red string, from a box on the floor.

"Is that all you need?" she asked.

"Yes, thank you."

The girl wrote down the items on a piece of paper for her records. Matias watched with curiosity, wondering how a yogi can manage a business and stay Zen all at the same time. It seemed to him that a person had to make a choice: career or spirituality. He thought that there was a complete communication failure between the two dueling worlds.

"How do you balance work life with yogi life?" Matias asked the girl. "Sometimes, I worry that having a job again will get in the way of my spiritual practice."

"We live in a world where we need money, and if you have no other source of income, then you need to work!" She said simply. "So many people use their work to define them- and they get so attached to their jobs that any demotion or loss of work makes them depressed and miserable. Go and work, but just remember that it's a means to get by, and choose to use it as an opportunity to practice forgiveness with the people you work with."

"I just thought enlightenment meant I'd have to live in seclusion in some cave somewhere and do nothing all day but meditate," Matias said. "I thought I would have to abandon my friends and family and surround myself with yogis and gurus if I wanted to keep the stillness in my mind."

The girl handed him a receipt for the items, and he took out his money as she continued: "Not at all. We're no longer in a time where you need to live in a cave by yourself to find enlightenment. In fact, the opposite is true. Enlightenment is best attained when you're surrounded by people, in the real world, because that is where we are bombarded with so many opportunities to use what we learn in meditation and readings, and we can actually apply the principles of forgiveness and oneness in our everyday lives."

"It's such a relief to hear you say that," Matias said. "Thank you."

Matias paid for the goods and just before he walked away, the yogi said: "Don't worry, you'll be back in the mountains of your country one day soon."

"How did you know?" Matias asked.

It was true- he had been dancing with the thought of home every night. If mountains could shed tears, then the tall rolling hills of Lebanon were surely crying for Matias' return.

"Your soul is singing the song of your homeland," she replied. "You're supposed to be here right now, but you'll return again. Even as your soul sings a song, it also tells a riddle- about a girl in a bookstore who waits for you."

Matias left the marketplace bewildered. He felt the power of his soul, which he now knew had a name of its own. Navtej Singh. As he said the name to himself, he felt its radiance. The boy was speechless and as he walked back to the ashram, he wept silently and his tears spoke the language of his heart.

When he returned to the ashram, he saw that the guru had prepared an area where he would perform the ceremonial ritual. On the floor, there was a tiny wooden foot stool with a bronze Tibetan bowl filled with water sitting on it. Pink and yellow rose petals floated gracefully in the water, their fragrance carried through the air. The boy was in the same ill state as before, and his mother was sitting beside him praying silently beneath her breathe as she stroked his leg softly.

Matias brought the turmeric and sage to the guru.

"Very good," the guru said. "Now make careful notes on everything that I do. Remember every detail so that you are able to repeat it to me if I ask you, understand?"

"Yes, master," Matias said.

The guru stood before his makeshift shrine, took a scoop of rose water and poured it into a smaller bowl. He then added turmeric and stirred the mixture until it became a yellow paste. He dipped his fingers into the paste and smeared it onto the boy's face and chest while chanting "sat nam, sat nam, wahe guru". It looked like some tribal ceremony where a boy was initiated into manhood, Matias thought. But he was careful to stay present and make a mental note of everything the guru was doing in case he would be tested on it later.

The great guru put the turmeric paste down on the wooden stool and picked up the bundle of sage, struck a match and lit the tip of the leaves until they released their intoxicating fumes into the air and filled the room within seconds. He waved the bundle around the boy's feet and the mother used her hands to guide the smoke toward her face-- just like she was splashing water onto her face, she basked in the sage smoke.

Suddenly the boy opened his eyes and stopped shivering. There was no slow response or agonizing wait like movies and general life experiences would have one expect; this was a plain miracle.

"Mama," the boy said. And he just smiled and understood what happened.

The mother showered the great guru with compliments and well-wishes and swore to devote her life to his teachings. The guru simply nodded his head and smiled, allowing her to say what she needed to say, but not allowing his ego to be flattered.

When the boy and his mother left the ashram to return home to their family, who surely was waiting in anticipation to know the boy's fate, the guru asked Matias to come close.

"Did you take note of everything I did to heal the boy?"

"Yes, guru."

"Can you repeat every single step to me?"

"Yes, guru."

"Good," the guru answered. "Now forget every single thing, I made it all up."

"Forget it!" Matias repeated. "What do you mean?"

"It was all an act, Matias." The guru said.

"Then why did you make me walk all the way into town to get turmeric and sage?"

"I thought it would add a nice touch," the guru said. "It was part of the show."

"Master, I don't understand," Matias said.

"People want miracles," the guru explained. "But they are not ready to accept them. Miracles are all around us, we just need to be open to seeing them. I performed the ritual with the turmeric and sage so that the mother and her son could accept the healing. They needed to *see* a physical remedy to believe in healing."

"If it wasn't the turmeric and sage or the chants and the ritual, then what was it?" Matias asked.

"It was a simple miracle," The guru replied. "To heal a person, you must see the light in them. The light is in everyone, but when they are sick, they are denying the light inside of them."

"What is the light?" Matias asked. "Where does it come from?"

"It is the part of yourself that you share with God," the guru replied. "I healed the boy by looking beyond the illusion of sickness that the mind created and glanced instead upon his eternal light. When you truly and wholly recognize that light in another person, you correct the error of sickness."

"So you're saying that the boy was never sick?" Matias asked. "It was just an illusion?"

"To think that a person can be sick is to believe that a part of God Himself can be sick, and *that* is insanity," the guru said. "An ill person has simply forgotten who she is, and she is asking for the love that would remind her that she is perfectly whole."

The next morning Matias took a stroll through town to see the city of Rishikesh with his newly cleared mind. Everything was the same, but entirely different. He had little thoughts. When he looked upon a person or situation, he accepted it for what it was and made no attempt to judge or interpret it. Everything was simply the way it was and he had no thoughts about them.

As he walked, he heard a painful cry coming from a ditch on the side of the road, and he stopped to see who or what produced the awful sound. There he saw a cat that had given birth to a litter of kittens not long ago, but was dying from lack of strength. The big Himalayan cat squirmed like a demon before a crucifix and pawed at the ground powerfully before it finally collapsed and seemed to give up all hope for the fight to live. "Now that's a painful sight," Matias murmured.

Upon seeing him come near, the cat was frightened for the safety of her newly born babies and raised herself with her front legs but immediately collapsed back down to the ground. Matias sat beside her and patiently stroked her fur until she became comfortable in his rhythm and her heart relaxed. Animals are instinctual and this one knew Matias was a friend. With every stroke, he said a prayer for the cat. He knew that he was one with everything and that included the cat; he was both the healer and ill. But he denied illness. Refused to see it.

"Divine Mother," Matias said. "Please lift from me, any thoughts that are causing this cat to be weak. Please erase all the negativity in me that is making her ill and as it is healed in me, it will heal in her, for we are one."

Saying the words meant nothing, meaning them meant everything. Matias saw the light of the universe within the cat and realized that even she was holy. To believe that she is sick was to believe that God himself could be sick, and to think that is insanity. He refused to see the illness. He denied the sickness' existence and simply continued to stroke the cat patiently until she finally stood as though her strength was restored and gathered around her children, licking them and tending to them with the strength of a mother. When she reclined on the dirt road this time, it was to feed her babies the milk from her tit, and Matias rejoiced in her health and returned to the home of his guru.

Matias was pleased with the evolution of his soul from a bitter barista fired from his job, a scared boy at sea, an angry person for having his money stolen from children of the slums, a new yogi in Amritsar and now a highly conscious yogi with the ability to heal. But fear was still lurking in the shadows of his mind and popped out from time to time to bring forth an unwelcome thought. Matias remembered the relic the ship captain gave him, promising it would relinquish the fear in his heart when he held it tightly. He took it out from underneath his pillow, where it sat forgotten since he arrived at his master's home. He held the silver relic in his hand and felt its coolness extend throughout his body. With closed eyes, he said, "Infinite light, please assist me in casting out any fearful thoughts and energies from my heart and help me experience the purity of my own soul."

And in an instant, the captain's promise was fulfilled. Matias not only felt his fears disappear, but also didn't remember what it was that he feared in the first place. It was a liberating feeling that would otherwise only have come with more years of meditation and clearing practices.

"Thank you my dear friend," he said to the captain, "wherever you are."

The great guru stood at the helm of Matias' room and asked if he could come in.

"Yes, of course," Matias said, ushering his master to sit with him.

"You are proving to be my fastest awakening student, Matias," the guru said. "You are close to drinking from the bountiful fountain of enlightenment, but you are lacking in some ways."

"Help me, master," Matias said. "I welcome your instruction."

"You need only to let love into your heart," the guru taught. "Love will do everything else that is required, all you need to do is let love in."

"But my heart is open," Matias said. "I love you unconditionally."

"You love with the body," the guru corrected. "You must love with your soul."

Matias leaned close and listened, as the wise master continued:

"When you love with your body, using your eyes and other senses to express love, you are putting a limit on love, because the body is always limited in its love. You say you love everything, but still see it as something that is external and living outside of you. If only you knew, that God himself is incomplete without you and your love. If you limit yourself to the kingdom of your body, then you will be a sad king. In your meditation let love come into your soul, and it will enter, because you came to it without a body and it was your higher self that invited it in. Love does not see bodies; it perceives the universe as a whole, and you are part of that whole."

Matias had the feeling, the knowing actually, that he *was* the universe experiencing life within a body. He felt a calm freedom from the body he identified with for so long. He still wanted to have a villa next to Jumblatt's and he desired the girl from the bookstore in Lebanon more than ever, but he didn't worry anymore about how we would get them. He was certain that divine mother would provide.

The Great Guru mediated alone in his room that night. He had been acting differently those last couple of days, but Matias thought it would be rude to ask him about it. It felt like his guru was no longer entirely there, disconnected in some way. But Matias didn't take it personally. One of the first lessons his guru taught him was to never take anything personally. If the master was acting differently, he had a reason for doing so- he was working something out within himself. Matias meditated alone in his bedroom. Even though he was tired, he struggled to keep his eyes fixed on the tip of his nose to stay focused on the present moment.

He suddenly saw the girl from the bookstore standing before him, in all her beauty. He wanted so badly to reach out and touch her cheek and tell her how much he's thought about her since he left his hometown. But she stood still and motionless like a songless bird, and paralyzed him with her solemn gaze. Then she spoke: "You left me here alone to go find yourself. You broke my heart" Matias knew that what she spoke were not waking words, but a different language- a language of dreams. He must have dozed off in his mediation. But it felt so real, like the kind of dream where you fall off a cliff and wake up with sore limbs.

The entire room was black and in the darkness, Matias reached out for the girl's hand, but as he did, she transformed into Raphael! He was red in the face and angry.

"I was supposed to be the Great Guru's student," Raphael said. "You took my place. You manipulated me!"

"You're the one who ran off with a girl!" Matias recanted. "I begged you not to, but you left me alone in a strange country."

Raphael didn't say anything back. His expression just became angrier and angrier until little green scales began to sprout from his face and he started to look like a reptile. The transformation gained momentum and he was suddenly becoming bigger and scalier until he was a giant fire-breathing dragon. Smoke fumed out from his nostrils and he opened his mouth and fire circled around Matias. He could feel the heat as beads of sweat fell from his face, but for some reason he wasn't burning. The fear however, consumed him. And the dragon began to taunt him, speaking in doubles:

"Holy! Holy!" It said. "Hello my sweet sweet. Did you really think you could be enlightened? You're just a simple simple barista." Then the beast breathed: "I see the fear fear inside you, stupid barista. Leave enlightenment to the gurus."

And as though he had been summoned, Matias' guru appeared before him in the dream.

"Matias, you are ready to receive initiation into enlightenment," the guru said. "You just need to release your fear of it."

"My Guru," Matias said, "all my life I've searched for God. Now that He is so close, I'm afraid, because I don't know what will happen to me if I become enlightened. Will I have to go live in a cave? Will I have to abandon my name and my dreams now that I know they are just illusions?"

"The only change you need to make is in your mind," the guru said. "Keep your dreams and keep your name. Just be detached from them and know they are only illusion. The days of having to live in a cave in order to be enlightened are gone.

The death of ego is not a death of yourself, but rather an awakening to your eternal self- your eternal truth."

Matias knew he was dreaming, but it felt like the conversation with his guru was real. It was as though the great guru penetrated the dream world and met Matias at the crossroads between illusion and reality, to divinely intervene between the boy and his ego mind. Standing barefoot and wearing nothing but his yogic garments, he looked directly into Matias' eyes and a veil of love fell upon his face. He looked at his student with an expression that offered complete forgiveness and his sins were suddenly dissolved. And as they melted away, there was the understanding that they were never there to begin with.

"Here is your purpose," the guru said, tapping Matias on the forehead to give him a vision of his destiny, "there peace awaits you."

Matias saw before him a premonition of fairytale proportion: He lived in a paradise and people traveled from afar to gather around him and hear his wisdom. And everywhere there was light.

When Matias opened his eyes, his guru was gone but his spirit was everywhere. The fire from the dragon evaporated into a cloud of smoke and then turned into a thousand roses that showered over Matias in divine blessing.

Thereafter, the light around him brightened. So bright that had it leaked out, there would be eternal sunshine even in the darkest corners of Earth. The dragon was gone. Matias' mind was silent. Rays of dancing lights swirled and twirled around him, little ballerinas doing a delicate Plié on the stage of awareness. And Matias hungrily drank that light like it were milk from a mother's teet. His grin became devilishly innocent. Saintly orbs circled around him, displaying peace in their orbiting. For the first time he saw the color of truth.

The light was there all along, Matias thought, he had just forgotten it. It was already imprinted on everyone, because God willed it so. It was just obscured by fear and hidden by the ego. Just like the sun is always blue. It's sometimes covered by clouds of gray, but beyond them, the sky is always blue. And the wondrous light Matias finally saw, corrected all the errors his mind had previously made.

The light brought with it an ancient memory of Heaven, and as it was restored to his awareness, it made no amount of sorrow or suffering possible in any form. Although Heaven knows no anguish, it offered him comfort. Even though it knew he already had everything as a child of God, it showered him with gifts. He rested in the light, untroubled; certain that only good can come to him, and any other who rested completely in the hands of the divine mother. He no longer entertained the belief that the world was his enemy, for he chose that he would be its friend.

Even time made more sense to Matias now. This instant he was enlightened. The next instance he might feel fear again. Only one more instant and he could face death. So he handed this very instant, and every instant thereafter, to divinity. Relinquishing control, he gained the power of the universe.

The dream must have lasted longer than Matias previously thought, because by now the sun was moving across the sky, like it was being pulled by an invisible little string. Daylight peeked its face into his room and smelling the scent of sunshine, he opened his eyes, unsure of what he would see before him. He was happy to behold that everything was the same as he left it. Only clearer. Newer.

Matias wanted to see his wise guru, who always happened to be up before him, no matter what time it was. He slowly got out of bed, dizzy and aloof with higher consciousness, and walked to the living area. His guru was seated in a meditative position, but opened his eyes upon hearing Matias' steps. They smiled at one another and in the moment that they stared into each other's eyes, it was understood that they shared a cosmic communication in the dream world. The guru held the stare a little longer, as though he were playing a game where the objective was to not blink, and Matias saw not only the universe, but also something he had been searching for all his life: God.

Matias sat next to his guru and rubbed his feet.

"Fear is a decaying tooth in the mouth of consciousness and last night you extracted it from your awareness," the guru said.

"I can feel all the miracles of God within me," Matias replied. "I am a magnet for them." He no longer felt like just a student of the master, but someone who could carry a discourse about spiritual awareness.

Discourse is not even the right word to describe it. There was no right word. There wasn't a word at all. Enlightenment can be explained poetically as 'a golden torch in a darkened cave' or 'the blissful sound of a flute swimming in the river of a guru's heart', but nothing compares to feeling enlightenment and experiencing the purity of a person's own consciousness.

"The dream reminded me of the girl from the bookstore, and how I was afraid to lose her, but now I know I will see her again."

"You will find her again if you are meant to," the guru said.

"And Raphael," Matias said. "He was supposed to come with me to find you, and the guilt of leaving him behind was holding me back from enlightenment."

"The boy still has a lot to learn, but he is on the right path. He is at least searching for truth."

"Before coming here, I thought God couldn't be reached directly," Matias said. "But now it's so clear that there is no space between God and his children. He is in everyone, because He *is* everyone."

"In this world, we can have a brief moment of direct contact with God," the guru said. "It is nearly impossible to keep the line of communication open for the entire time here, although some have attained it."

"You're one of them," Matias said.

"Yes."

"So this moment will pass for me?"

"Don't despair, for just like you came from light, you will one day return to light. Until then, you will always have the memory of being in union with the creator, and that will keep your consciousness elevated."

"Thank you," Matias said. "You guided me to this state of awareness."

"I only awakened what was already dormant in you."

"What do I do now?"

"Go back to your home, and teach what you have learned. It is written on your forehead to be a teacher. Remember that when you speak to those who are suffering, speak their language so they can understand you. Speak about suffering even if you feel no anguish. And for every problem they bring to you and every problem you have, ask for the answer and wait, it won't be long. And do not question the answer when it comes."

"And what about you?" Matias asked. "Will you stay here?"

"There's nothing left for me here," the guru said. "Helping you on your path was the last of my karmic duty in this lifetime."

"So you're moving to another place, or..."

"No other place. No more places, Matias. In this lifetime, I've seen every life I've ever lived. In some, I lived in caves and others I spent in palaces. I'm done with the endless cycle at last."

"So you're going to die?"

"Like all souls, mine is eternal. But upon death, the soul leaves the body, just as owls abandon a falling tree. I was supposed to depart the body the day I met you, but when you came to me, I knew I needed to help you reach this state before leaving."

Matias wanted to beg and plead his master not to leave him, and to stay in his bodily form just a few more years, perhaps come to Lebanon with him. But it was so clear that the guru was ready to go. He had already transcended life and death and that's why, Matias realized, the guru had been distant over those last few days.

The guru looked at Matias and smiled lovingly, but more than just lovingly. It was a smile that reminded a person of his purity and made him forget all the bogus beliefs of this world. It stopped time, and not in the cliche way that people use the phrase, the minutes literally stopped and there, the past could not reach them and no thoughts extended toward the future. In the innocence of a smile like that, one became a child again, transformed from an adult who longs for things and fears the world, into a child who laughs in the face of ego.

"Can I ask you one more question, great guru?"

"Anything," the guru replied.

"What's the point? Why do we even come here at all?"

"Because it's fun," the guru laughed.

Matias smiled. He loved the witty answers his guru gave to some of the most serious questions.

"Nothing this world sees is true. It's all a dream in the context of the frame you created. It's only purpose is to be a place where those who have forgotten who they are can come to question who it is they are, until they eventually remember their soul and their creator once again."

"How long does it take to remember the truth?" Matias asked.

"For some it takes thousands of lifetimes," the great guru answered. "A person will come back again and again until enlightenment is reached and they accept that it is impossible to doubt their true self and to not be aware of who they really are."

The great guru had reached the atonement he spoke of. His breath would soon leave the body, even as a family of horses abandons a field that lost its grass, and he would be off to wherever it is everyone comes from. Heaven, some would call it. He would go back to his nature and become one with everything again- the winds of the Himalayas and the flight of a hummingbird.

"My time with you has been brief, master, and the conversations even more so, but you leave me with a richer heart and a stronger spirit," Matias said.

"Even though death will hide me, my truth lives in you to teach to others."

"What has been given me during my time here I will keep," Matias promised.

Nothing else was said, for no formalities were needed. Matias carried his silence and began the journey back home to the mountains of Lebanon. He heard the ancient cedars of his homeland calling out for his return. Before leaving, he chanted a quick "Aum Namo Narayana" in honor of his guru, which is traditional for Hindus to do when death looms over a loved one. It was not necessary in this case, because he and the guru both knew that the master was not dying, only changing, merging with the eternal. Still, Matias thought it would be fitting.

As Matias waited for the train, he dug his feet into the soil of Rishikesh one last time, feeling its warmth blanket his toes with the eternal life force. He wanted to remember the soil when he was long gone and carry its memory with him.

It was on the train that he noticed for the first time how different his energy had become. He sat in a seat across from a mom and her two young children. They fought and screamed as siblings do. But when Matias sat across from them, a silence fell upon them and they shyly bowed their heads down a bit and huddled close to their mother. It was like a humbled thief before the pope. An older man with clearly very little to give, approached Matias and covered his lap with a blanket to keep him warm. He bowed his head and walked back to his seat. Matias was living with the great guru for so long that he was unaware of the energy he was radiating from within. In India, where people are aware of gurus and spirituality, most people can recognize a highly conscious person when they see them. The trip out of Rishikesh was much different from the one in; he sat silently and unaffected by either illusions nor the ego's tricks.

When he arrived at Delhi, it was exactly as he left it when he first arrived from Lebanon. A loud city, with crowds of people everywhere, yelling and talking, making deals and rushing from corner to corner. It frightened him the first time, but now he saw himself as a centered being of calm energy in the middle of a tornado.

And then part of that tornado spoke in a familiar voice.

"Matias?"

It was Raphael.

"Matias," he continued, "I had a dream last night that I would see you today."

He was alone, with the girl he left Matias for nowhere in sight. He was almost unrecognizable wearing a disheveled beard and a mask of sadness. In the time since he left Matias, he became nearly penniless. The nomad had always enjoyed playing card games, and realized during his time in Delhi that card games were more fun when money was involved. The contrast between the two young men was undeniable. Once they were both naive and searching for truth together. And now one was lost and fallen astray from the path, and the other an enlightened young man on the way back to his hometown to fulfill his destiny as a teacher of truth.

"Hello friend," Matias said. He was still thankful to Raphael for pushing him to embark on the path that led to discovering truth. Nor did he judge the nomad as good or bad or lost or found; he simply was.

"I'm still searching for God, you know," Raphael said. "I just got a little distracted, but that's how life goes. I met a lot of very spiritual people here too, so it wasn't like I was wasting time." He felt the need to explain himself, but he was uncomfortable, because he was speaking with ego and Matias was speaking with spirit, and there was a complete communication disconnect between the two.

"You hold the power of God, my friend," Matias replied. "Let go of the idea that your thoughts are powerless. Everything you see and experience is the result of your thoughts. There is no defense against this truth."

Raphael was like a child before Matias' new energy. Matias was a mirror reflecting Heaven onto Earth. He made Raphael wonder, and long to be better. He reminded the nomad of who he really was and what he could become if he focused.

"I take it you are returning home?" Raphael asked.

"Yes, it's time for me to return."

"That's great," Raphael said. "You've clearly found what you were looking for, and now it's my turn to do the same. I'm heading to Rishikesh today to finally meet the great guru."

Matias remained still and unaffected hearing the name of his master. He didn't tell Raphael that the great guru he was searching for had already departed his body, because he felt it was not his place to interfere with Raphael's life path. The wind blew to the West and Matias turned his head to the East, and he heard the wind whisper to him, "The nomad needs money for his journey". Matias had enough for a flight to Lebanon and gave the extra cash to the nomad to take a train to Rishikesh. At first Raphael tried to be polite and deny that he needed any help, but he couldn't be untruthful with his enlightened friend and eventually accepted the money humbly. The formerly partnered seekers of truth embraced one final time and went on their separate paths.

Matias purchased a plane ticket to Lebanon using money from the gold coin the police chief sent him while he was in Rishikesh. On the journey back home, Matias thought about his destiny to teach all the universe. He knew that everything he thought or spoke was connected to everything. He was not alone in anything. It was his destiny to change every mind along with his, for he was the mirror that reflected the power of God.

*

The first place he wanted to visit when he arrived in his hometown was the bookstore. It was where he found the book that started it all, and where a special girl was waiting for his return. But something kept him from going there. A feeling. Not now, he thought. But soon.

He did go to the coffee shop, though. The familiar smell of coffee filled his spirit. He recognized most of the customers, but they didn't seem to recognize him immediately. The once nicely-dressed beardless barista was now a yogi draped in white garments with an unshaved face. Most unrecognizable though, was his spirit, which was new; a mirror reflecting truth.

He went to the counter to order a cup of Arabic coffee, and met the barista who replaced him: a younger boy, perhaps seventeen. And in him, Matias saw himself.

"Are you a yogi?" the boy asked.

"I am," Matias replied.

"My grandfather is a sheik, and he told me about people in India who study with gurus until they merge with God," the boy said. "Are you a piece of God?"

"Yes," Matias replied. "And you are a part of God, too. We all are."

But the boy couldn't see himself so divinely. Across the counter, the coffee shop owner had not changed much, and he still didn't tolerate distractions at work. He abruptly interrupted the conversation.

"Shadi!" he screamed at the young barista. "If you spend all day talking to each customer, we will never sell any coffee!"

Matias was unmoved. He looked into the owner's eyes and there was only forgiveness in his gaze. The past was not there.

"Matias--" the owner's voice broke off into nothingness. "You look different. What are you a Sikh now?" He laughed.

"Call me Navtej, old friend." Matias said. "The name of my soul is Navtej Singh."

The owner recognized that there was something different about the boy he once ordered around like a dog. He was not the same person, but born anew. The owner felt embarrassed in his presence, as though Matias could hear the negative thoughts within him. He felt naked, his soul undressed and revealed.

"I've thought about you a lot since the day I fired you. I wanted to say that I'm sorry. You were loyal to me for years."

"The past is a dream," Matias said. "You only see the past, and it keeps you from this moment right now."

Then Matias lifted the coffee cup that Shadi, the new barista, had served him by now. And he continued:

"Take this cup of coffee, for example. Instead of seeing it for what it is, you see only past experiences of drinking, of being thirsty, of feeling the warm coffee touch your lips. All your reactions are based on past experiences with cups. And when you look at me, are you doing the same thing? Are you thinking about a boy who worked for you, and a boy you feel guilty for hurting? Forget all that. See me as I am right now. Let's have a new experience right here in this moment."

In that moment, all was forgiven. Matias showed the coffee shop owner that he had become immune to attack. And he taught the owner that he is guiltless and it was impossible for him to cause Matias any harm. There was nothing to forgive. By refusing to allow the shop owner to think he can attack, Matias taught him that salvation was his just as much as it was Matias'.

And suddenly the shop owner's face, whose brow had been scrunched for years, softened. He saw Heaven in Matias' eyes and begged permission to follow him and be his student. He wanted to go to the boy's home, and even offered to be his personal barista in exchange for the secrets of happiness.

"I'll freely share everything I've learned," Matias said, "but what you gain is up to you."

"I'll follow you now, then."

"Not right now," Matias said. "I'll go home and settle in and then my door will be open to you and anyone else who needs guidance."

"Allah khaleek," the owner said. It meant "Good keep you" in Arabic.

On the walk home, Matias made a stop at the bookstore to see the girl he thought about often since he left. He no longer had ego-thoughts so he didn't wonder what it would be like when he saw her, he didn't make up illusions of all the things that could go wrong, and he didn't think about what he would say when he saw her.

Things looked different inside. The music before was gentle; classical and instrumental. Now, French rock played from the speakers around the bookstore. Matias sensed that the energy of his *friend* was not there.

A college-aged boy stood at the cash register. He was a trendy artist type with long black hair sleeked back with hair product. He wore a plain white shirt and skinny black jeans.

"Bonjour," he said.

"Bonjour," Matias replied.

"Can I help you find something?"

"No," Matias said. "Well yes, a person not a thing. The girl that works here, or used to work here. She had brown hair, sad eyes..."

"Ah, Selma."

Selma, Matias thought. Beautiful name.

"Yes, is she here?" Matias asked.

"Nope. She went to Bali. Said she met a customer here who inspired her to go on a spiritual journey or something."

Matias was surprised. His tongue was tied up, but he wasn't upset, because he knew in his heart they would meet again. And when we do, he thought, we'll have so much to talk about. Lifetimes worth.

Unlike the bookstore, his home had not changed at all, aside from the dust that had gathered neatly on the surface of everything. As Matias ran his finger across the dining room table, he thought he should donate everything except for the bare essentials to charity. There was a community center in town that Matias always wanted to help in some way. They provided books and after school activities to local kids who didn't have much otherwise. They could benefit from the extra furniture, and he could use the material freedom.

Elias Ajram came to Matias' home with a team of volunteers from the community center to pick up the furniture Matias wanted to donate. Elias was the center's manager. His family, well known in town, donated the center to the city generations ago, and were known to use their money for philanthropy; unlike the Jumblatts who used their wealth to expand their property and power. Matias used to respect that about the Jumblatts. Now he wished they would see how much wealthier they could feel by giving a portion of their fortune to the needy like the Ajram family did. Matias knew Elias since they were little children. They used to walk to school together and Elias was never one to gossip. That was a rarity in this Lebanese town, where gossip was a form of popular entertainment.

"Matias... I mean Navtej, sorry, habit," Elias said. "Are you sure you want to give all of this away?"

The world saw giving as losing something. By giving it away, it was lost. But Matias saw it as a gain for himself, and he gave in his own self-interest. He did it for himself, and not the self the world identifies with, but his higher self.

"I'm sure," Matias replied.

"It's just that it's been in your family for years."

"And now I hope it will serve the community center for generations, just as it's served my family," Matias answered.

"It will," Elias assured.

As the volunteers hauled the furniture outside, the two old friends spoke about life, naturally. Matias didn't like to teach with words, because he knew that to really teach is to demonstrate. But sometimes people spoke and they wanted to hear answers, so Matias obliged.

"I thought yogis were just in India," Elias commented.

"No, they're everywhere," Matias replied. "And not all yogis look like me: white clothes, a head wrap and a long beard. A yogi is simply someone who seeks truth."

"Do you think meditation would help my anxiety?" Elias asked. "The center is a big responsibility and sometimes it makes me stress. It's hard to sleep at night."

"When I worked at the coffee shop," Matias demonstrated, using himself as an example, "I used to spend so much time aligning all the coffee cups in straight lines after they were washed. Everything had to be perfect. Each row had to have eight cups and all the handles had to face left. It wasn't just ritual, it ran my life. I don't think about those things anymore. The compulsiveness just melted away. That voice that directed me before was replaced with light."

The verbal part of Matias' teachings were really secondary. The relevance was showing Elias what it meant to be assured in the truths of the higher self. And what Matias gave, he received for himself.

"There's a gentleness about you that wasn't there before," Elias noticed. "That's proof enough for me that what you're doing works."

Matias only smiled. He felt his destiny was being fulfilled, be it slowly.

"Can I join you in meditation sometime?" Elias continued.

"Any time you like," Matias said.

He took a look around his empty home after the volunteers left, and was pleased with the simplicity. He found fullness in the emptiness. He kept only a couple of couches and chairs for his guests to sit on. He didn't know how seekers would come, but he knew they would. In his bedroom, only the bed, a side table, and one armoire remained. on top of the side table, he placed the book that started it all: Sat Nam - Healing Kundalini Yoga.

It wasn't long before word got around in the small town about the boy named Navtej Singh who returned from the far east with enlightened thoughts. Remember that gossip was a common pass time in the town and Matias didn't mind as long as it brought people to him. Those who were meant to learn something from him, came. Winter arrived quickly, and in the mountains of Lebanon, it brought with it snow and cold. People prepared for months by stocking up on foods and logs for their fireplaces. It was the only way to get through the winter. But none of those things kept people away from visiting Matias. They went to him seeking answers to their problems. Even the town psychics came to see the boy who was taking away their business of telling fortunes, and they were surprised that he was giving people answers and joy without pretending to predict their future, rather he told them that they created their future with their present thoughts. And they found it even more surprising that he didn't charge any money for his time. He only accepted donations for food and necessities, or a donation to the community center.

"You could be making a lot of money," one psychic told him. Dollar signs filled her wide eyes.

"And then what?" Matias asked.

"Then you could open your own office where people come to see you." She replied.

"And then what?"

"And then you can hire a staff to run the place for you and you would just sit back and see people who paid for appointments."

"And then what?"

"Then you would have enough money to open a franchise of offices across the country where people can pay to come in and listen to your teachings. And you wouldn't even have to be there. You can hire people to teach your teachings for you!"

"And then what?" Matias asked one final time.

"And then you can have enough money to live a nice, peaceful, quiet life in the mountains with simplicity and enough time to meditate and drink tea and paint whenever you wanted."

"That's my life now," Matias said.

He taught the business-minded people in his hometown that they could attain a life of peace and happiness right in that moment. He often heard people say, "I'll be happy when..." and I'll be happy if..." and he showed them that they could be happy *now*. All that was necessary was a willingness to be happy.

The garden in his backyard was small, and it didn't take long for it to be full with guests every day. Matias would meditate for hours every morning when he woke up before the sun rose, and then sit in his garden and see guests one by one. The majority of them were mothers worried about the future of their families, and sheiks who wanted to know the answers to all the questions prayers didn't answer.

One afternoon, after seeing three mothers and four sheiks, someone else came in to see his advice.

It was the first time Matias had seen Monsiour Jumblatt since the day he was fired from the coffee shop years before. Jumblatt looked like he'd aged much faster than a man should, and it seemed like he had a wrinkle for every dollar he had ever earned. The only thing that didn't change was the Italian suit he was wearing. It was fresh. New. Expensive.

"I came to personally see the man I've heard so much about from the sheiks," Jumblatt said. "Where are you from?"

Matias smiled, realizing that the preoccupied millionaire didn't even recognize the boy who'd served him about four hundred cups of coffees years ago.

"Don't you recognize me?" Matias asked.

"No," Jumblatt answered. "Should I?"

"Who makes your coffee these days?" Matias asked.

"How should I know? The boy at the coffee shop, my servants..."

"For four years, it was me." Matias said.

Jumblatt's eyes squinted, like he was remembering some ancient memory.

"Ahh yes," he said. "I noticed you left when I suddenly stopped having roses drawn into the foam of my cappuccinos."

They both laughed.

"So that was you?" Jumblatt asked. "The enlightened barista."

Matias nodded.

"I have so many questions for you, let me take a look at my schedule here-- we'll make an appointment --"

Jumblatt took out his planner and started to skim through it with his pen.

"How is the 14th for you?" He asked.

Matias stared at him blankly. Here was this millionaire who sought truth and sat before a man who could help him reach it, and all he could think about was his schedule.

"I don't think about the 14th, or any day in the future. How about right now?" Matias asked.

"Now?" Jumblatt said.

"What questions do you have?"

"Well, I guess I have time for a quick question," Jumblatt started. "Maybe you can tell me this: I've worked hard my entire life and amassed a nice fortune. So why aren't I happier?"

"The Earth is always giving to us. We have flowers, water, air, mountains to hike and oceans to swim in, but we seek more. And in that seeking, we find things to buy and sell. And in that buying and selling, some are left with wealth and others poverty, some become greedy and others become hungry. But when you give and receive love, there can be no winner or loser, everyone wins. Don't stop your business, but try having love in everything you do. It'll be hard in the beginning, but after a while, love becomes the theme of your life, and joy must be present wherever love is."

"That's good," Jumblatt said. "That's really good. See- that's what I need. I'll tell you what- I want to build you a villa next door to mine. That way you can always bless the Jumblatt family and you'll come over and teach my children everything you know. What do you think?"

The universe was offering Matias the very thing he always wanted as a youth. My villa next door to Jumblatt, Matias thought. But there was a word in that thought he didn't like to say: my.

"That's very kind of you to offer, but..."

"We can start building immediately, you could move in by Summer."

Matias knew that to keep and protect anything, a person has to give it away. Whatever he gives, he receives. Love is giving, and in order to have love, he had to share it with the town and the world. Keeping it to himself and denying the gifts of truth to the world, he would be keeping it from himself as well.

"I'll accept on one condition," Matias said. "Let it not be my villa, but let it belong to the people of Lebanon and abroad. A sanctuary where those looking for answers may come to learn the lessons I would place neatly on the lap of humanity."

"Deal!" Jumblatt said.

He put out his hand for Matias to shake. The only thing Matias wanted to shake was his head, but he humored the seasoned businessman and obliged him with a nice firm handshake.

*

FIVE YEARS LATER

The sun's brushstroke painted the sky yellow. Then orange. The sun was pleased to burn. It burned with no motive other than to light the world. And as streaks of blue prepared to come in, Matias was coming out of his morning meditation.

People already began to form a line in his garden. They carried offerings for the man who by now was nicknamed "the enlightened barista" not just in Lebanon, but all over the world. It was ironic and somewhat unfitting, considering he hadn't brewed a single cup of coffee in years. Nevertheless, it was his job as a barista that set him on his path to enlightenment in the first place. Monks from Tibet, priests from Spain and everyday seekers of truth gathered in his villa next door to Jumblatt's in search of something bigger than their awareness. Some brought him money and others carried presents, but most offered bowls of oranges, which Matias in turn handed out to his guests while they waited for their turn to see him.

Matias knew they were meant to be his students. They were born to be his students and he was brought there to be a teacher to them. When he accepted his role, they filled their part and came to learn. The universe had it all planned and orchestrated perfectly, he thought. What Matias did for them, really, was take them back to an ancient time when their souls were free and before they created illusions out of fear. Back to a time when they were light. And as they remembered it, even if for an instant, they awakened to what it was they really were.

He began as he always did, by introducing himself to the crowd:

"Hello friends, I am Navtej Singh. Or Matias, as my mother would have liked for me to be called."

As he spoke, the crowd looked less like living things and more like lifeless toys, so still as not to miss a single honeydew word from the barista sage's mouth.

"It is believed that there is a level of peace that is beyond this world, but can be attained in this world. But where is it? How is it found? Through giving it away. When you give peace away, you receive it for yourself. Give hate, and it will cling to every part of your life. When you hate, you deny the existence of peace. Therefore you won't find peace. Please- be soft, be peaceful, and make yourself comfortable. I hope to speak with each of you today."

By now, he was quite comfortable with his role as a teacher of truth. He always knew what to say and what people needed to hear from him on their path. He also had help coordinating the crowds of people. Both the coffee shop owner and Elias Ajram devoted most of their time to helping Matias by lining people up in the morning while he meditated. They picked up all of the offerings and cut the oranges into slices to serve to the anxious clusters of guests. Matias was so pleased to see how much kinder and gentler the coffee shop owner had become. He even adopted a new dog, which helped to light the torch of joy that hid darkened within him for so long. Now he was never seen without a smile on his face and the whisper of peace upon his brow.

Not everyone was as devoted or accepting of the enlightened barista. There were those who believed Matias was a magician who contradicted their religious beliefs and that his healing of the ill were mere tricks and illusions. But his followers devoutly defended him, saying that it was the illnesses themselves that were the illusions.

Matias' villa was sometimes vandalized by his naysayers. Every morning someone would write "sinner" on the large glass window on the front of the house, and each morning Elias had to wash it off. As luck would have it, Jumblatt had a security camera put up long ago, so the coffee shop owner and Elias knew it was the grumpy old Sheik Imad who was marking the window. He was unapologetically open about his hatred for Matias, but he never admitted to vandalism. When the coffee shop owner and Elias told Matias they knew who it was, Matias did not allow them to confront the sheik. In fact, he instructed them to show extra kindness to him and not allow him to think he can do anything to hurt them.

"Let him see that you are invulnerable," Matias said. "And that he too is invulnerable. He cannot do anything to make us deny him his place in the kingdom."

It was too everyone's surprise, everyone except for Matias, that on this particular morning, Sheik Imad was first in line to see the enlightened Barista. He kept his head down and made it clear he didn't want to be seen.

Elias noticed the sheik while he served oranges to people waiting in line and he remembered Matias' instruction to treat him with extra kindness.

"Sheik Imad!" Elias welcomed him.

The sheik uncomfortably looked around with his beaded eyes, to make sure no one heard Elias.

"Yes, yes, hi," he responded.

"Please take an orange," he said. "It's a blessing from Navtej Singh."

"No, no, I don't like oranges," Shiek Imad said, shooing the bowl of fruit - and Elias- away.

He was first to see Matias and he didn't waste a second going inside to the private room and out of the public's sight. He held his head down before Matias, embarrassed for all the gossip he'd spread about him in town, but also unsure if Matias had heard any of it.

"Hello, brother," Matias said.

He knew everything the sheik had said about him, for though he never asked, the townspeople were quick to tell him when they came to seek his guidance. He also knew that Sheik Imad was responsible for the vandalizing of his window every morning. But Matias was beyond such petty things, and he didn't take any of it personally, because he knew that everything the sheik did was not because of Matias, but because of something he was dealing with internally; Fear and hate raged together like a storm within him.

"Hello," the sheik replied. "You know, people say a lot of thing about your teachings, but I never partake in it. I know that we are all children of Allah."

"Yes, we are," Matias said. "What can I help you with today?"

"I am a religious man already and don't really need any teaching, but I do need your help with something else."

"Anything I can provide," Matias said.

"I know you get a lot of donations, and I heard that sometimes you help people who need money. I built a large home for my family. It was my wife's dream house. But I can't make the final payment this month. If I don't come up with the money, they'll take it all away from me- the home I spent three years building."

"How much do you need?" Matias asked.

"Five thousand dollars is my final payment."

"I'll have Elias arrange it for you in the morning," Matias promised.

"Praise you Navtej, praise you!" The sheik said. "I knew you were a good man, I told everyone you were."

"And you can't even see my demonic horns," Matias said jokingly.

"Oh, you heard that I called you a demon..." the sheik said. "That was a joke, of course, I make a lot of jokes!"

Matias raised his hand to quiet the sheik.

"I also know you are fond of calling me a donkey, but I should tell you- if you stay on the path you're on, it will take you twenty lifetimes to even reach the conscious level of a donkey."

Now the sheik was truly embarrassed.

"I try not to gossip," he sheik said. "But it's in my nature. Is it really that bad?"

"God gave us the power to create; the power of the word. When you use the word to gossip, you are not only hurting the person you gossip about, but you hurt yourself. Whatever you give, you receive for yourself. And the person you gossip will hate you for attacking them. Do you see the poison you brew?"

"Yes, enlightened one, I'm beginning to see."

The Sheik took Matias' hand and thanked him profusely for the money and the wisdom, then headed for the door.

"And Imad..." Matias said.

The sheik stopped and turned around.

"Take an orange on the way out. It's good for you."

The sheik nodded and smiled.

Elias came into the room after the sheik walked out.

"How'd it go?" Elias asked.

"I don't think you will be washing any more windows," Matias laughed.

"Ready for the next guest?"

Matias nodded.

A nun came in. She was young and pretty, with eyes wide like a baby fawn. She sat on a pillow-covered wooden bench across from Matias and he took her hand lovingly.

"Thank you for seeing me, enlightened one," she said with meek devotion. "I've traveled a long way to see you."

"What are you seeking?" Matias asked.

"I am conflicted between two challenging ideas," she said. "I joined the convent, because I know it is my path, but I also find it hard to believe that peace is possible in this world. I feel like there's no point to all the work we do feeding the needy and defending the helpless. It doesn't seem to change anything. Is peace possible?"

"God has already promised peace, so it must be here," Matias said. "He promised that there is no death, only change, and he promised happiness to those who ask for it. We can't make the world peaceful or dangerous, we can only choose how we look at it. You and I might look at the same tree and one of us would call it ugly and the other beautiful, but the tree is neither of those things. It just is. Whether we see it as beautiful or ugly only reflects what we are feeling on the inside."

"So the world is peaceful as long as I judge it so?" she asked.

"Don't judge it at all, that's the point," Matias replied. "The universe has already determined that the world is peaceful and there is no death. It's your judgment on it that condemns it to be dangerous and declares that death is inescapable. The universe cannot be wrong in its thinking, so you must be. Release your judgments and the world will be released along with you."

"Should I keep helping others or is it a waste of time?" The youthful nun asked.

"Keep helping. Offer peace and it will be yours."

The line outside began to get longer and in order to make sure everyone had a chance to see the enlightened barista, the coffee shop owner had to rush people through quickly. The next person to see Matias was a veteran politician who apparently had sought the meaning of justice his entire life, and had not yet found it.

"Laws are so complicated," he told Matias. "Politicians make laws only to break them like gusts of wind erasing a declaration written in the sand. How can there be justice this way?"

"Politicians don't know what justice is, because they think it lives in chains and jails," Matias said. "True justice is undoing the errors in our minds. You think it takes a powerful man to put sinners in jail, but I say a powerful man is one who can say 'I am truth. I am light. I am a child of God, for I am a thought in God's mind.' In Heaven, there is no justice, because there is no injustice to begin with."

"And here on Earth?" The politician asked.

"The closest thing to justice here is forgiveness," Matias said. "No law and no politician can give me justice. That comes from God alone. And His justice is salvation, wholly without judgment and fully free of condemnation for any 'sin' we thought we committed."

"I just want to put all those little thugs in jail," The politician admitted.

"Instead of trying to put all of them in jail, why don't you focus on getting yourself out?" Matias said. "Accept freedom for yourself."

"But I've never been in prison."

"You think you're free?" Matias asked. "Let me ask you this- why did you become a politician?"

"If I'm answering honestly, it was to make my parents happy," he paused. "And to impress women."

"When you worry what others think about you, you become their prisoner," Matias said. "When you act in a way that serves someone else's agenda rather than your own, you trap yourself in their chains. And when you see people as nothing but little thugs, then you see them as just a body, which must mean that you see yourself also as just a body- therefore you imprison yourself. Set them free from your judgment and you too will be free."

The politician smiled politely and said he understood everything, but Matias could see that he was not convinced. The ego was strong in this one. But his soul was gentle and willing to learn and that would serve him well on his life path. The politician was however relieved from the burden of bestowing justice on his own, and for that he made a generous donation to the community center and left with a smile on his face.

It seemed the whole mountain, even the weeds and the ladybugs, paused to hear Matias' wisdom. Everything that is, except for the sun. It shifted across the sky like a theatre curtain, and like the end of a show, it finally brought with it the darkness of a finale.

The last person in line was a clean man dressed in unblemished white clothes from head to toe. He came late and it was normally not customary to take late arrivals.

"I'm sorry, I was in surgery all day," the man explained. "My patient had a tumor the size of a grapefruit growing out of her thigh."

"How did she put pants on?" Elias asked. He pictured this woman walking around with a big goiter on her side.

"She wore dresses," The doctor replied.

"Like big dresses or regular one?"

"Regular ones, I think," the doctor said.

"What color was it?" Elias asked.

"Forget about the tumor for a second!" The doctor said. "Can I see the enlightened barista or not?"

"Yeah, yeah come on, I'll take you in."

Matias was playing with an old watch when the doctor walked in. He enjoyed taking things apart and putting them back together.

"Come in," Matias said. "Have a seat anywhere you like."

The doctor sat down and Matias beside him.

"I always stay a bit later after everyone has left, because someone always ends up walking in a little late," Matias continued.

"Thanks," the doctor said, "I was in surgery."

"Ah a doctor," Matias said. "I suppose your question is about healing?"

"How does healing happen?" The doctor asked.

"You tell me," Matias said. "You're the doctor."

"But that's medicine and surgery," he responded. "How is *real* healing accomplished? The kind you do."

Matias held up the watch he was fixing as it ticked and tocked the time every passing second.

"The only way I am able to fix this watch, is by finding out what is causing it to stop in the first place," Matias said. To heal, you need to recognize what purpose the illness has. Illness comes from the mind, so the mind must have a purpose for having created it."

"I don't know..." the doctor said. "Why would a person create illness in themselves?"

"Because for some reason the person sees value in the suffering. The ego is cunning enough to convince the body that it is dying, and in that dying it thinks it is strong, because somehow it killed itself before God could kill it," Matias replied. "I know it's a difficult idea to understand, but once a person no longer sees any value in their illness, healing can take place."

"What can my patients do to promote healing?"

"I find that affirmations can be useful for most people," Matias answered. "Keep treating them with medicine, but have them also say 'I have no use for this sickness, it offers me nothing and I am healed' - and watch your business begin to suffer."

The doctor laughed. "That would be a happy suffering," he said.

"Remember, if your patient thinks he is sick, he must believes that God Himself can suffer."

Using his words, Matias stuffed a hook down the doctor's throat and pulled the belief in sickness out of him. Piece by piece, petal by petal, he deflowered the darkness and replaced it with truth.

And as the doctor left the villa, Matias was happy to see another person come in. The one who always came in after everyone had gone for the day. The one who grew more beautiful every day. She was radiance wrapped in grace.

And as always, she had a book in her hand.

"How was your day?" Matias asked.

"I closed the bookstore early and took a walk. Yours?"

"I saw the light in a lot of people today."

The girl from the bookstore sat next to Matias and took his hand. He played with the ring on her finger, lining up the diamond with the creases in her knuckle, thinking about how lucky he was to have married a girl who was aligned with him.

A nightingale flew in through one of the open windows and sat on a wooden bench beside Matias and his wife. Nightingales were his favorite bird. They weren't made of metaphors. They were simple and forgiving. The winged beauty cocked its little head to face Matias. He looked into its eyes, and saw his guru staring back at him. And as the bird's eyes gazed back, they seemed to say *Sat Nam*.

END

Printed in Great Britain
by Amazon